THE FORGER'S DAUGHTER

THE FORGER'S DAUGHTER

AN IRIS REID MYSTERY

SUSAN CORY

ISBN 978-1-969756-02-3

"You can look at a picture for a week and never think of it again. You can look at a picture for a second and think of it all your life."

JOAN MIRO

CHAPTER 1
AN EMPTY STUDIO

I ris Reid had known what to expect when she had moved in with her chef boyfriend Luc over a year ago. But being together 24/7 last month while on vacation in Costa Rica made it difficult to come back home to their mismatched schedules.

She faced another Saturday evening with only her dog for company. Sprawled out on the living room sofa with several *New Yorker* magazines at hand and a ham sandwich halfway to her mouth, she jumped when the intercom chirped.

Iris wasn't expecting company, and Luc was downstairs in the restaurant kitchen orchestrating one after another James Beard award-winning meal for the Paradise's appreciative fans.

The intercom video screen showed Luc's son, Ash, shivering in the February cold at their downstairs entry door. Sheba, Iris' Basset hound, jumped off the sofa and positioned herself in the hall, ready to greet or repel the visitor.

After she buzzed him in, Ash climbed the stairs to the loft. He peeled off his threadbare wool coat and tossed it over the handrail. Ash had his father's height and the same blue eyes, but darker skin from his mother. His dreadlocks were swept back in a ponytail. "I should have called first." He glanced at the half-eaten sandwich in Iris' hand and groaned. "And I'm interrupting your dinner."

"Don't worry. Have you eaten? I can make you something."

"No, I'm good."

He looked anything but *good* standing in the hall frowning, his hands jammed in his paint-splattered jeans pockets.

"Let's go into the living room." Iris motioned him to a chair.

Ash launched right in. "Do you remember the woman you met in my building last week? The painter who rents the studio across from mine?"

How could Iris forget her? A pre-Raphaelite beauty who, no doubt, inspired fervent poetry writing from dreamy-eyed young men. The type of woman who projected fragility but was probably tougher than she looked.

"Sure. Wasn't her name Luna?"

The woman had been leaving Ash's painting studio as Iris entered, and he'd introduced them. Iris was there to drop off some leftover glass tiles. She'd been the architect for renovating the abandoned brick-making factory he'd bought with an inheritance from his stepfather. Iris had converted it into four artist studios for him and several tenants.

"Right, Luna Esposito. She's missing. I think she's been kidnapped!"

"Wait, whoa,—hold on. What makes you think that?"

"We were supposed to meet for dinner last night. She never showed up." Ash glanced away from Iris.

He'd been dating her goddaughter, Raven, for over a year and, as far as Iris knew, it was getting serious. *Why is Ash having dinner with this woman? Are they just friends? Is he going to break up with Raven?* "Maybe Luna forgot and went away for the weekend."

"I tried calling her. No answer. I knocked on her door and it was open."

"Unlocked or actually open?"

"Open a few inches. Her cat was roaming around in the hallway."

"Did you look inside? She wasn't sick or passed out?"

"No. Her purse was on the bed, and her coat was on a hook by the entry. And she still hasn't returned any of my texts."

Iris felt the familiar spark of unease and curiosity twist together. As an architect, she'd learned to solve problems, and this scenario did not sound good. "Maybe you should file a missing person report with the police."

"I tried this morning. The cops said it hasn't even been twenty-four hours. She's an adult, and there's no evidence a crime's taken place. She probably thought she had closed the door before going off somewhere."

"Did she leave food and water out for the cat?"

"No. I brought him into my studio for now."

"Maybe she took some credit cards and her phone and forgot her charger?"

Ash dropped his head into his hands. "I don't know! She's just gone. I know she's in danger. I have to do something." He looked up at her. "You told me how you tracked down that woman who was stalking you. Iris, please help me."

CHAPTER 2
THE GIRL WITH THE PEARL EARRING

On Sunday mornings, Iris and Luc usually slept in. Since the restaurant was closed that day, Luc could skip his early morning trips to the food purveyors and focus completely on Iris. At least, that was her perspective. When they eventually made it out of bed and wandered into the kitchen, Iris mentioned Ash's visit and his request for her help.

Luc waited for the fancy cappuccino frother to finish whooshing before he asked, "Why can't he go to the police? They're the ones who locate missing persons."

"He tried that," Iris called from the dining area as she set the table. "They told him Luna was an adult and had probably gone off for the weekend and forgotten to tell him."

"Maybe that *is* what happened. Sounds like he's overreacting."

"Luna left her studio door open and the cat alone without food or water. And she was supposed to meet Ash for dinner that evening."

"Wait—isn't this woman just his tenant? Why is Ash so worried about her?"

Iris carried their large cups of coffee to the table. "I think Ash has a crush on her. I met her last week, and she's very attractive."

"But he's dating Raven. I thought those two were serious." Luc buttered the sourdough toast and carried a plate over to the table.

"I thought so too. As far as I know, Raven is planning to move in with him this summer after she graduates."

Luc swore under his breath. "Oh, boy. Do I need to have a father-son talk with him about how to treat women? I don't want him hurting Raven."

"Let's not jump to conclusions. It seems premature but I promised, if she wasn't back by tomorrow, I'd look around Luna's studio to see if there were any clues about where she may have gone. I'll also try to suss out the level of Ash's involvement with her. This might just be concern for a friend. Anyway, he and Raven are adults."

Luc cocked an eyebrow.

"Well, sort of adults," Iris conceded. "I'm not sure their romantic arrangements are any of our business."

"Tell that to Ellie if Ash breaks her only child's heart. If you get any confirmation that Ash is interested in this Luna character and you don't share that with Ellie, it could damage your friendship."

Monday morning, as Iris drove to Ash's once-dilapidated factory, she admired the building's elegant new look. Even if she *was* the one responsible for it.

Ash met her at the front door. "Still no word from her."

Iris gave him a solemn look.

Inside the tall space, large wooden trusses supported an exposed plank roof, punctuated by glass solar tiles that let in diffused sunlight. The well-worn brick floors served as a reminder of the building's original utilitarian function. Ash slid his master key into the lock of the unit across from his own.

Luna's studio mirrored Ash's own, with large industrial steel windows covering the top half of the outside wall. Eight large canvases were propped up against the perimeter of the big open space. Each of them featured dark, brooding slashes of paint, mainly in black and grey. The paintings were all basically abstract, but Iris sensed something ghostly lurking behind the surface layers.

"Some powerful art, huh?" Ash sounded admiring. "Luna calls this series *Prisoners*."

"Curious choice of title." Iris wanted to know more about this woman. "Do you have any photos of her? I may need to show them around."

"Luna was weird about getting her picture taken. But I do have one on my phone. I was taking a shot of one of my paintings, and she was in the background. I can print it out for you." Ash glanced around the room and sighed deeply. "It's hard for me to be in here with Luna gone. Do you mind if I go back to my studio? Tell me if you find anything, okay? Thanks again for doing this."

Ash left, and the door banged shut.

So much for Luna being just a friend. Damn.

Iris approached a large unfinished canvas set on an easel in the middle of the room. She squinted. Most of the canvas was bare, except for some violent black brushstrokes in the upper corner. Then, in a lower section, a delicate image of a woman's face in three-quarter profile had been carefully rendered, the size of a dessert plate. It looked totally out of place with Luna's other abstract pieces. Iris moved closer. The woman's yearning stare and half-opened lips looked familiar. Iris suddenly thought of her father, who had been a professor of art history at Dartmouth, and it came to her. That face unmistakably belonged to the young woman in Vermeer's *Girl with a Pearl Earring*.

7

Why was this modern artist inserting a literal face into her piece, and a copied image from a classic Old Master painting at that? It was a damned good replica. Iris took a step back to see the whole canvas. Maybe Ash could shed some light on the meaning of these two juxtaposed styles.

A quick inspection of the other canvases in the room failed to turn up any similar anomalies, although she had an eerie sensation of something lurking beneath the thin layers of paint.

She shook her head. *Enough art appreciation. Time to get down to business.*

Iris looked around for a desk, but the only pieces of furniture in the room were a beat-up wooden table and chair that looked like they had been salvaged from the sidewalk, an unmade daybed and an old bureau. Iris fished through the table's drawers but found nothing of interest: an electric bill addressed to Luna Esposito from last month, some scissors, a hammer, random pencils and pens, printer paper but no printer. The table surface held the expected artist's tools: brushes, oil paint tubes, a palette crowded with dabs of different colors along with a palette knife encrusted with dried paint.

Where was Luna's computer? She must have a laptop somewhere. Iris made a quick circuit around the studio but couldn't spot one. Was this woman a Luddite as well as a minimalist?

Moving closer to the kitchenette, Iris caught a whiff of a sharp, piney odor. An open cup of turpentine holding several paint brushes sat in the sink. Good brushes were expensive and shouldn't be left soaking for long. Iris was finding it harder and harder to believe that Luna had left her studio intentionally. She checked the cabinets and refrigerator for hidden clues, but they only contained a small collection of plates, glasses, and a skimpy supply of groceries. Luna sure wasn't throwing any large parties.

As Iris returned to the main room, the hair on her arms prickled.

Sensing that someone was watching her, she looked out the wall of windows, searching for someone looking in. Other than several slow-moving cars and a few innocuous-looking pedestrians, no one was focused on her. Still, if Luna was taken from this studio, it might be dangerous to be seen rifling through her things.

Iris walked back to the easel in the center of the room. Vermeer's *Girl with a Pearl Earring* was definitely eying her. She approached one of the finished paintings propped up against a wall. Studying it, she made out another set of eyes. Yes—another face was buried under surface washes of paint. Moving from painting to painting, she identified images from other famous Old Master paintings hidden in all the canvases. These haunting images must be her prisoners. It gave Iris the creeps.

She continued her search. A daybed was pushed up against a wall. Partially hidden in the messy folds of the bed's duvet, Iris spotted a leather tote bag. Was this Luna's day-to-day purse? Another bad sign to find it left behind. Looking inside felt so invasive, but if Luna was in danger, snooping might save her life.

Iris dumped its contents on the bed. Her purse contained a wallet, lip balm, a wadded-up tissue, sunglasses, a small hairbrush, and apartment keys. No cell phone. Iris opened the wallet. It held forty-three dollars in cash, some change, and a Charlie Card for the subway in a separate pouch. No ID, credit cards, or anything else with her name on it. What a woman kept in her purse often revealed who she really was. Given this, Luna was a woman without an identity.

She appeared to be living off the grid. How was Iris supposed to track down someone like that? Had Luna's enemy found her, and she'd run to escape? Better that scenario than if she'd been abducted.

Iris felt a faint ridge of something inside the wallet pocket. She slid in a finger and maneuvered out a small piece of cardstock. It was a studio portrait of a three- or four-year-old boy, posed against a stack of giant alphabet blocks. He had dark hair and eyes and a timid smile. The photo was dog-eared from handling. Who was this child, and how was he connected to Luna? Maybe Ash knew.

Iris took a photo of the boy's picture with her phone and placed all its contents back inside the tote bag.

She checked under the mattress and cushions on the daybed, then looked through Luna's meagre wardrobe of T-shirts, jeans, and a few dresses spread between the closet and the bureau drawers. Iris dipped her hand into various pockets, but found no clues secreted away. The exercise made her want to pare down her own overstuffed wardrobe. She found a large, battered duffle bag shoved into the back of a closet, but without any old airline tags that might suggest previous travel. Luna might have had another suitcase she'd taken with her.

The medicine chest and vanity in the bathroom were no more illuminating. What was Iris expecting to find? A receipt for a bus ticket, a pregnancy test kit, wadded up threatening letters from someone, a hidden shoebox, a matchbook with the name of a restaurant? Unfortunately, this wasn't a TV show.

Iris took a last look around before leaving Luna's studio, noting the parka still on a hook by the entry. Nothing in those pockets. She crossed the hall and knocked on Ash's door. As it opened, an enormous ball of brown, black, and white fur shot past her legs, almost knocking her over.

CHAPTER 3

A CAT NAMED KEVIN

"Kevin, get back here!" Ash stood in the doorway glaring at the obese cat scratching on Luna's door. He scooped Kevin up in one strong hand and gestured Iris into his studio. "This is her cat. I'm stuck with him for now."

"And you told the police Kevin's water and food bowls were empty when Luna disappeared? That didn't get their attention? Guess they're not pet owners."

Ash dumped Kevin on the floor. The cat strutted over to the front door, narrowing its eyes back at Ash.

"He hates me."

"One more reason to find his owner quickly."

"For what it's worth, no one from the cops even came by to check out her studio."

Ash picked up a paintbrush he'd left by his easel and wiped it on a rag. "Let me get you some coffee. Sit down and tell me what you found." He moved over to the neatly organized counter of his tiny kitchen while Iris sat on a stool nearby.

"I didn't know what to make of her big canvas with the Vermeer girl's head," Iris said.

Ash half-smiled as he filled the espresso pot. "Did you notice that all her paintings have images from Old Masters?"

"I figured that out."

"She overlays them with so many thin coats of paint that you can barely see the faces unless you know they're there. Art schools teach you need to learn to draw figuratively before you can be a good abstract painter. Luna's riffing on that idea, having these figures imprisoned under abstract layers. At least I think that's her point."

Ah, symbolism and semiotics. Some architects play those games too—claim their buildings have all sorts of hidden meanings that go over the heads of laypeople. Iris considered it mostly BS. But she had to admit, Luna's paintings did have a weird, menacing presence.

The coffeepot sputtered, and Ash poured the dark, aromatic liquid into two glass mugs. He added a splash of milk to Iris' before sliding it across the counter to her. "Did you find any useful clues?"

Iris turned her eyes away from admiring the celadon backsplash tiles she herself had chosen for these kitchenettes. "Luna's purse was still there. The brown leather tote. It has her wallet and keys inside."

"See—she never would have left that behind!"

"I agree. It doesn't look like she took a planned trip." Iris took her phone out of her pocket and scrolled to the photo of the boy. She turned her phone toward Ash. "I found this photo in her wallet. Do you know anything about this little boy?"

Ash lifted the phone to look closely. "No. Why would she have this? The only family she mentioned was an uncle from Revere, who she listed on her rental form. I tried calling his number, but the line was disconnected. She never mentioned anyone's kid."

"Can you show me her lease?"

Ash moved to a file cabinet next to his desk and withdrew a form. He handed it to Iris. "I know I should have done more background checking. But I thought another painter would be a nice addition to the studios. We already have a tenant who builds mixed-media constructions and a graphic designer." He stared into his coffee while she quickly scanned the sheets.

Iris handed them back. "Luna carried no ID in her wallet, no credit cards. How did she pay her rent?"

"Cash. I figured she must have a side gig that paid her under the table." Now Ash did make eye contact. "I guess I suck at being a responsible landlord."

"No, it's fine." Iris said. "Just makes it a little tougher to track her down. Any idea where she might have worked?"

"She never mentioned an employer. I'm just guessing. Her money could've come from waitressing or maybe an inheritance from a parent. I don't think she'd sold any of her paintings on her own, and she didn't have a gallery yet."

"You said you had a picture of her?"

Ash went over to the printer sitting on an old wooden desk and came back with an image on glossy paper.

The photograph featured one of Ash's colorful expressionistic paintings displayed here in his studio. Off to the left stood the ethereal woman Iris had met. In this picture, she looked beautiful in the way of precious metal—cool, hard. Her curly red hair reached the middle of her back, and her eyes were the green of absinthe. Luna wore a paint-splattered jumpsuit and seemed to be lost in thought, unaware of her image being captured.

"It's hard to believe someone this striking wouldn't be easy to spot," Iris said. "Once we pass her photo around, I'm sure someone will have noticed her."

"She would stuff her hair up in a cap, wear sunglasses and a ratty raincoat to dumb-down her looks." Ash smiled sadly. "Never worked though."

Iris could guess why he'd accepted her as a tenant with minimal screening.

He went on. "She kept to herself and didn't have much interaction with the other two tenants, but you can try talking to them." He glanced toward Luna's studio. "One afternoon, I got Luna talking about her art, and that's when she started to open up a little. She's so talented."

Iris sipped her coffee and stared at the photo. Who was Luna Esposito? She was clearly living off the grid. Was she hiding from someone dangerous? Or maybe *she* was the dangerous one, a con woman hiding from the police. Judging from her art, she seemed haunted by demons of some sort. Did they catch up with her last Friday and spirit her away? Or did she make a run for it?

CHAPTER 4
A NEEDLE IN A HAYSTACK

Iris drove back to Cambridge with three tentative leads: a photo of Luna, another of an unidentified boy, and a possible contact—her uncle's name and town, assuming that wasn't made up. Even with those, she had no idea how to track down this mysterious woman.

Ash's parting words to Iris expressed his faith in her. "I really appreciate your help. Luna must be in danger, and I know you've found people before. Tell me right away what you discover."

Right away. Needle in haystack. How did she get this rep? She was an architect, not a P.I. With that thought, she headed to her office to check on her two employees and her actual day job.

The office of Reid Associates was located in a Cambridge single-story former furniture store, with large plate-glass windows facing the sidewalk. Iris parked and entered. Her office manager/mother hen, Loretta Jackson, sat at the front reception desk talking into her Bluetooth headset. As she spotted Iris, she held up a finger. "I'll get back to you with her schedule soon, Jason. We're all looking forward to the wrap party." She looked up at Iris, one eyebrow raised.

"Wrap party?" Iris moaned. "Will this hell ever end?"

"You're in the home stretch, Hon." Loretta took off her headset. "Jason just needs to tape you giving a last tour of the finished museum, delivering a few inspirational words, and then the documentary's wrapped. Milo swears the punch list will be done by the time Alex Harcon flies in on Friday for the ribbon cutting. Then you can finally kiss your film career goodbye."

"I don't know how I let Alex talk me into letting this crew film the museum renovation—such a bad idea."

"He is the client. And a charmer. Plus, I can show you the fat performance fee they just deposited into our bank account." Loretta rapped a multicolored nail on her touchscreen monitor. "When should I tell Jason you'll do the final taping?"

"Why don't you co-ordinate it with Milo for Friday and put it on my calendar? Thanks."

As Iris moved into the open-office space, she saw her architect Rollo Baptiste collecting black line drawings from the large-format printer. His dark curly hair was getting long. The new father wouldn't have time for haircuts these days.

"Hi, Rollo. How's the baby? Sleeping through the night yet?"

"I wish."

"Where are we with the Brewster Street schedule?"

"Milo submitted the permit application and final plans last week. I'm working on shop drawings now for some of the built-in cabinetry. Do you want to see them?"

"How about after lunch? I have a few things to do first."

Iris went to her office, closed the door, and sat down at her desk. Her new firm was running just fine without her. Eight months ago, Reid Associates had been a one-woman operation. She had done everything, from finding projects to designing them all the way up to the structural drawings and supervising the construction. Now she was beginning to feel superfluous.

That wasn't true. She still needed to find new projects to keep everyone busy.

But first, she fumbled through her purse for her cell phone and called Luc. He picked up on the first ring.

"Luna's still missing, and it looks like she left in a hurry."

"Willingly?"

"I think something unexpected caused her to run, or else someone nabbed her. I didn't find any ID in her wallet. Looks like she's been living off the grid."

"She sounds shady. I don't like Ash being involved with her."

"Or maybe she's the victim." Iris described what she'd found in Luna's apartment—the abandoned cat, the picture of the boy, and the lack of detail on the lease she had filled out.

She could hear Luc chewing something on the other end of the line, no doubt an ingredient for some recipe he was experimenting with in their kitchen. Iris doodled a face on the notepad on her desk.

Luc finally said, "If the local cops don't want to get involved, Ash should try to get the FBI to look into this."

"Short of someone receiving a ransom note or Luna having a prominent family connection, I doubt they'd be any more interested than the police."

"Do you think we can get Ash to let this go?"

"He seems pretty torn up about her disappearance. I said I'd try to follow up on a few leads. I doubt I'm going to find anything. This woman has put a lot of effort into hiding her identity."

"Okay. But I don't want you taking any risks. Luna could be involved in something dangerous."

"This legwork should be safe. Since the restaurant's closed

tonight, maybe you can help me with the search. We can get it over with that much sooner."

"Okay. Give me an assignment."

Iris realized that the face she'd drawn resembled Luna's. "Why don't you try tracking down Luna's uncle from Revere?"

"Sure, I can do that. Give me whatever contact info you have for him. Maybe Ed can help."

"Great idea. And while you're at it, see if Ed has any advice for how to find a woman who's been living under the radar."

Ed Rostow had been his father's partner back when the two men were detectives on the Cambridge police force. Luc's father had died under tragic circumstances many years ago, and Ed had recently retired.

"I wonder if I could learn anything new by showing Luna's picture around the Medford neighborhood. Ash thinks she might have had a side gig, maybe waitressing. Someone might even recognize the little boy in the photo." Iris looked down again at the face she'd drawn on her pad. "And I'll text you the photographs of Luna and the boy in case anyone in Revere can ID them. FYI, Luna might not be her real name."

"I figured." Luc paused. "Did Ash mention anything about Raven? Do you know whether they broke up?"

"He didn't say a word about her, and I'm still not clear about what's going on between Ash and Luna. He seems protective of her, but she just might elicit that reaction in general from men."

After Iris ended the call, she thought about Ash's dreamy expression when they'd talked about Luna's looks, and she anxiously chewed on her thumbnail, a bad habit she'd quit a year ago.

Iris spent the next half-hour on her computer searching various sites, typing in Luna's name repeatedly. She knew this would not be the way to find her. It was just the quickest way of confirming that.

Once Iris had run out of useful websites, she scanned Ash's photo of Luna into her computer's photo archive and cropped it to show just the woman herself. Iris printed it, along with the photo of the boy. Staring at them side by side, she noticed they both had large, deep-set eyes, although his appeared open and innocent while hers looked like they had some miles on them. Were they related? The boy didn't live with her, so he was unlikely to be her son, but Luna had kept his picture close at hand. Was it even recent? There had been no studio name or date on it. She returned to the browser and did an image search of the two faces. When that yielded no results, she searched for commercial photography studios in the Medford and Revere areas and printed out the addresses of the two listed.

Iris rose and stretched. It was becoming clear that her afternoon would be eaten up with this wild goose chase. She needed to talk with Ash's other two tenants, who hadn't mixed with Luna much, but might have noticed something relevant. She added that to her to-do list, which included showing Luna and the boy's pictures around the neighborhood and trying to find the correct photography studio. Maybe someone would recognize the boy from a playground or a toy store. He looked well-fed and decently dressed, so someone was looking after him. She added these ideas to her list.

When Iris passed through the open office again, Rollo looked up. "Want to go over the drawings now?"

"Can you send the PDFs to my computer? I'll review them as soon as I can," Iris said. She waved to Loretta. "I'll be on the road this afternoon. Call if you need me."

CHAPTER 5
THE OTHER TENANTS

Iris parked in front of Ash's building and entered the chilly center hallway. Strains of an opera aria escaped from the studio next to Ash's. She rapped loudly on Ash's door, hoping he could hear her. She should have called first. He was probably absorbed in painting.

After a few moments, the door jerked open. Ash's eyes widened. "You're back. Do you have news already?" Kevin the cat shot past him again and threw himself against Luna's door, all the while emitting piteous yowls.

Ash hauled the unhappy cat back inside his studio, closing the door quickly behind Iris as she scooted in. Kevin jumped to the floor and stalked off to the kitchen.

"Not yet," Iris answered, "but I'm going to show these two photos around the neighborhood. I'd also like to talk with your other tenants. I hear music coming from one of the studios. Would it be okay for me to knock on their doors?"

"I saw Reilly here earlier, but Jess went skiing for the weekend and I don't think he's back yet."

"Jess is the one whose studio is next to Luna's? He might have seen something out his window. Their places both overlook the parking lot."

"Yeah. I'll introduce you to Reilly next door, and I'll keep an eye out for Jess."

It took several minutes for Reilly to hear Ash's knocking. The music stopped abruptly. An Asian woman with short red hair, shaved on one side, answered. "Oh, hey Ash. Was my music too loud? Sorry about that." She laid down the power drill she was holding on a nearby table.

"No, it's not that. This is Iris, a friend of mine. We're trying to find Luna. Have you seen her since last week?"

Reilly darted a look at Iris, sizing her up. *She's wondering if I'm Ash's cougar,* Iris thought.

"Luna's missing? Are you sure she didn't just take off for a break—maybe go someplace warm?"

Iris and Ash stood in the hall, but Iris could see large chunks of various materials behind Reilly. It looked like a junkyard. She had to be the tenant who built big mixed-media constructions.

"We were going to meet up last Friday, but she's disappeared," Ash explained.

Reilly shook her head. "Can't help you. She keeps to herself. We sometimes pass in the hall, but it's not like we're buds. I haven't seen her for a while. But I remember her damn cat raising holy hell in the hall last week."

"When?" Iris asked.

Reilly thought for a minute. "It must have been around four on Friday because I was just leaving for work at the Dirty Dogma." Seeing Iris' questioning look, she clarified. "It's a bar over by Tufts."

"Did you ever see Luna around the neighborhood or working a side job somewhere?" Iris asked.

Reilly shrugged. "No, sorry." She edged the door closed.

Iris and Ash parted ways in the hall so she could get on with her search. She left her car in its parking space in front of the studios and followed on foot the map she'd sketched.

Her first stop was the nearby Healthy Planet, a café where she and Ash often met while his building was being renovated. Iris realized she was hungry and, after carefully scanning the crowd, headed for a small table in the back. Ash's mother, Luc's high-school girlfriend, lived in this neighborhood and often came here. Luckily, there were no Zoë Kravitz look-alikes that Iris could see. She had reasons to avoid her, and vice versa.

A pale server with long blond hair and no makeup wiped down the table and took a menu from her apron pocket.

Iris waved it away. "May I have a tuna sandwich and a glass of iced tea, please?"

"Whole wheat or whole grain, sprouted rye or flax seed bread?"

"Whole wheat."

"Lettuce, tomato, vegan mayo? It's made with soy."

"Yes, lettuce and tomato. Regular mayo is fine."

Before she could recite the litany of teas, Iris added, "Peppermint tea."

While Iris waited for her meal, she took the photo of Luna out of her tote bag and laid it on the table. When her server returned with her food, Iris turned it to face her. "I'm trying to find this young woman. Have you seen her?"

The server set down the plate and glass and looked. "She comes in now and then. Are you saying she's missing? You a P.I. or a cop?"

"No, just a friend trying to help. Do you remember the last time you saw her, either here or anywhere else?"

The woman frowned in thought. "I've only seen her in the café and not recently. I work eleven to three, Wednesdays through Saturday. She might have come in on my days off."

"Did you ever see her in here with anyone else?"

"Sometimes she comes in with Ash Burke. He's friends with the café owner and leaves big tips."

Iris retrieved the photo of the boy from her purse and set it on the table. "If you've got another second, have you ever seen this boy, either with the woman or with someone else?"

The server picked up the photo and studied it. "Cute kid. No, I've never seen him, sorry." She slid back the picture and turned toward another table.

Iris took a bite of her sandwich and stared out the window at the cars stopped at a traffic light. As she chewed, she tried to imagine how big a threat it would take to force her to give up her life in Cambridge, her life with Luc, her career as an architect—to live in hiding: getting paid under the table, having no ID, driving license, or credit cards. She couldn't imagine it.

CHAPTER 6
BASIA-PREVIOUS FRIDAY AFTERNOON

Basia Sobieski closed the book and looked down at the sleeping boy. His head rested against her side in the tiny bed. With a thumb in his mouth, he clutched a stuffed bunny with his other tiny hand as he napped. She was responsible for most of this child's daily needs, and she'd grown to love him like a grandson. She called him Pawel, Polish for Paul, or sometimes Misiu, which meant little bear. He called her Nana.

Paul already knew the book about the hungry caterpillar by heart and would pretend he could read the words. But Basia had only recently started teaching the three-year-old the alphabet. And since English was her tentative second language, she was not sure how good her lessons were.

Basia gingerly eased herself to her feet without waking the boy. She placed the book back on the small pile of toys she had brought along when they had made their escape. It would not do to be spotted buying children's things if Malik was still actively looking for them. That man had eyes everywhere.

Pawel's mother, Celia, had stopped by that morning, at her

usual time, to spend an hour playing with him. She had brought along some groceries: more pork for kotlets, dumplings that were a poor substitute for real pierogi, and a carton of milk. Basia wasn't inclined to do much cooking in the tiny kitchen of this rented studio.

Remaining as a "nanny" in the Boston townhouse where Malik was running his illegal operations was risky. By the time Basia figured out what was really going on, she had tried to find a way to escape. But Malik had taken her passport and made threats against her family back in Lublin, Poland, if she exposed him. Sure, Basia felt sympathy for the young mother, but she had only agreed to help Celia and her son escape because of her ever-growing love for Pawel.

This arrangement here in Medford was temporary. Celia was waiting for their new identity papers to arrive through an art school connection. Unfortunately, that kept them within striking distance of Boston. But Celia did not trust the process of acquiring new papers from an unfamiliar source for the three of them. Celia would pick up their new passports, licenses and social security cards in-person this weekend. Then, they could leave for California to start a new life.

Celia had promised Basia that she could live with them as Pawel's alleged grandmother, to remain a part of his life. After all these months together, Basia could not imagine how either she or Pawel would cope with being separated.

A scraping noise at the front door caught her attention. Glancing down at the bed to make sure Pawel was still asleep, she tiptoed to the entry and looked through the peephole. What she saw made her whip around and race toward the burner phone on the coffee table.

But she was too late.

CHAPTER 7

THE PHOTOGRAPHER'S CLUE

It was barely four o'clock, but the sky was steel gray, promising snow. Iris had covered most of the commercial streets of West Medford on foot, stopping at every place Luna might have worked, shopped, or spent any time. No one was able to give Iris any information beyond a few unhelpful past sightings, vague in the details. Showing the boy's photo had been equally unsuccessful. Few people were outside on the playgrounds in this weather, and the owner of the single toy store in the neighborhood hadn't recognized the child from the photo.

Iris was on her way back to the car, trudging down Sagamore Avenue, her feet cold and tired, when she noticed a small sign next to a doorway between a twenty-four-hour laundromat and a liquor store. It read: Gilday Photography. This place hadn't shown up in her online search. Through a glass-paneled door, she could see a dimly lit vestibule with a staircase beyond. Iris pressed the buzzer labeled Gilday and the front door clicked open. She stepped in. From overhead, a man's reedy voice called out, "Second floor."

The door at the top of the stairs was cracked ajar with a slit of bright light visible. Iris knocked on the jamb and entered a long, narrow room. An elderly man looked up from an old-fashioned contact sheet, strips of small images printed from photographic film he'd been examining on the counter, his magnifying loupe in his hand. "Can I help you?"

"I hope so. I have a studio photograph of a young boy, and I'm wondering if it might have been taken here." She placed it in front of him. Trying to ignore the man's nasal whistling, Iris glanced around the room and recognized a stack of alphabet blocks from her photo. They were assembled against a backdrop of seamless paper rolled onto a stand. A reflector, a bank of lights, and an empty tripod were set up across from it.

The man picked up the photo, then set it back down and eyed her thoughtfully. "I believe I did. This is the background I often use with the young kids. Why are you asking?"

Iris took out the picture of Luna from her purse. "I'm actually trying to find this woman who's missing. She had the photo of the boy in her wallet, and I'm hoping that if I find him, I can locate her. Luna Esposito. Do you recall if she brought the boy here?"

The photographer stroked his chin as he studied Luna's image. "No, no, that's not right. An older woman brought him in, I think. It was a few months ago. The boy was very well-behaved. They aren't always, you know. He seemed sad. I remember having trouble coaxing that smile out of him. They came in for passport photos, but when the boy saw the blocks, his face lit up. I convinced the woman to let me take a few shots of him with them."

She was finally getting somewhere. "What do you remember about the woman who brought him in? You must have her credit card and a phone number on file. Did she come back later for prints?"

The old man hesitated. "Why did you say you're looking for this person?"

"I'm a family friend and agreed to help search for Ms. Esposito. She's in great danger. The police don't seem to be concerned." *Okay, she might be exaggerating.*

The photographer hesitated.

"The boy may be in danger too."

Mr. Gilday moved to the computer at the other end of the counter and sat on a stool in front of it. He tapped the keys for several minutes before he looked up. "Here we are."

Iris joined him to look at the monitor. It showed a receipt for forty-two dollars for two sets of passport photos and no charge for a contact sheet of the boy's formal shot. The record noted that the client had received the passport photos at the time of the sitting. A note at the bottom of the screen said the client never ordered any enlargements of the studio shot, just kept the contact sheet.The lines on the invoice for the name, address and phone number were blank. The form stated: Walk-in. Paid cash for passport photos.

"Is this common for someone not to leave contact information?" Iris asked.

The old man shrugged. "It happens. As long as they pay, I don't pry."

Iris tried to keep the frustration out of her voice. "Can you tell me what the woman looked like? Did you keep a copy of her passport photo?"

"Not my policy to keep the passport ones. I've got no room to store them. As to what the woman looked like..." Mr. Gilday cocked his head. "Ordinary. But she had some kind of accent. Older than you, younger than me. Average-looking. Brownish-gray hair. I think she wore a kind of leisure suit. Is that what they call them— matching pants and a top? But the boy was dressed up nice, like you see in the photo. I was focused on him. Dress pants and a holiday sweater. Looks like a Christmas sweater, but we took the shot in early November. Maybe the picture was for a present. But she never ordered anything."

Iris thanked Mr. Gilday and left him a business card with her cell phone number written on the back. "If you remember anything else about them, or if you happen to see either one of them in the neighborhood, could you call me, please?"

As she turned to leave, the man blurted out: "Paul. If that helps, I think I heard her call the boy Paul."

CHAPTER 8
THE BLACK AUDI

The snow was falling heavily by the time Iris made it back to her car. As she reached for the door handle, her phone beeped with a text from Ash:

< Jess just got back if you're still around and want to talk to him. >

What she really wanted was to sit in front of her fireplace with a hot, alcoholic drink, but she turned back toward the studios. Given that Kevin was a known flight risk, Iris avoided stopping by Ash's place first. She texted him:

< I'm here. Will knock on Jess's door. >

A young man held the door open a crack, giving her a quizzical look. "Can I help you?"

"Hi, I'm Iris Reid, a friend of Ash's. We're trying to find Luna. No one's seen her since last Friday."

Jess opened the door wider to let her in. He appeared to be in his early twenties and wore a pair of hip black glasses with his puffy snowboarding overalls. A huge duffel bag stood in the middle of the room, random clothes spilling out the top. "I just got back from a ski trip, so I don't know how I can help. Luna and I weren't exactly friends."

Compared with her glimpse of Reilly's place, his studio looked tidy. Two monitors and a keyboard took up most of a large desk. The table next to it held a camera and a few neatly stacked sketchbooks. Jess was the graphic designer—no paint or turpentine in here.

Outside the large studio windows, the snowfall intensified in front of the yellowish streetlights which lit the small parking lot. "Did you see her at all on Friday afternoon?"

"Let me think. You want anything to drink?"

"No, thanks."

Jess hummed under his breath as he wandered over to his small kitchen and peered into the refrigerator. He scanned the contents, then closed the door. "My ride picked me up on Friday around four, so I would have been finishing up some work and packing my snow gear that afternoon."

Iris followed him, her stomach growling. It had been hours since she'd eaten a sandwich.

"Wait. It was kind of weird. Reilly was playing her music loud, as usual, but I thought I heard someone knocking on my steel window frame, like muffled pounding. When I went to look out, I saw a guy turn away from Luna's window and walk back to his car in the lot. So, I guess he'd been outside her studio, not mine, trying to get her attention. Right after that, I heard Luna's door swing open. She ran down the hall and out the back door to the car, screaming something. I couldn't hear what. She didn't even have a coat on."

"Angry screaming or happy screaming?"

"Sounded pissed off to me."

"What happened next?"

"I don't know. My ride texted, and I left out the front door. I noticed that her damn cat was in the hall. I figured Luna was coming right back."

"What did the man look like?"

"Um." Jess squinted his eyes in concentration. "He had on a black raincoat and a knit cap. I just saw him from behind."

"Anything distinctive about him?"

"You mean like tattoos? This was from the back, and he had a hat on, so I couldn't see his head or body. He didn't move like a young guy, so I'd guess he might have been around your age."

Iris tried not to grimace. "Thanks. How about the car?"

"An Audi SQ8 with tinted windows. Black."

Iris went to the notes app on her phone. "You certainly know your cars. Any chance you got the plate?"

"No, but I think I saw a face looking out the back window."

CHAPTER 9
A DESPERATE CALL

Ash tried to ignore his buzzing phone, lit up brightly on the stool behind him. He'd just filled his brush with a big dab of cerulean blue and wanted to complete the expressionist face flying over rooftops for his Allegory series. Oh, hell. It was probably time for a late lunch break now anyway, so he wiped off his brush. He didn't recognize the number on the caller ID but pressed the green button to accept the call.

"Yeah?" he said in a you-better-not-be-a-spammer-tone.

"Ash." The word came out in a whisper. "It's Luna. I need your help."

His heart jumped in his chest. "Where are you?"

"I'm —" Her words stopped abruptly.

"Luna? Luna—can you hear me?" Ash strained to hear any background sounds or voices. "Call me or text if you can. I'll find you."

Then the line was dead. He immediately called the number back, but it rang, then was cut off. He tried sending a text. The screen read, "Message could not be sent." WTF? Ash slumped onto a stool at his kitchen table. Kevin eyed him from the floor. Ash imagined someone tearing the phone out of Luna's hand. He knew it. She was in trouble. His mouth was suddenly bone dry, and he could barely swallow. His chest even ached. Was that his heart?

He had never meant to get involved with her. It started out with casual conversations in his studio or hers about their work. She had a deep understanding of art history and where she saw her work fitting in. Her mastery of conventional figurative painting was impressive. The way she combined it with abstract art was truly original.

Over the past month, the more they talked and traded opinions about art, the more passionate the discussions became. Their debates spilled over into film, music, and dance. To each of them, the arts were related in one creative continuum. Stirring up all that emotion, it seemed only natural that the two of them would become physically stirred up as well. And that connection also turned out to be on a different plane than Ash was used to.

But he already had a girlfriend. He loved Raven. It's just that she was such an innocent girl compared to Luna. Raven could be flighty and immature, and that was starting to get on his nerves. Even her paintings were less sophisticated than Luna's, or his own work for that matter. They had been dating for a year and a half and had been discussing Raven moving in with him after she graduated in June. Recently, he changed his mind about taking that step.

Ash wanted to be upfront about his feelings. Over the last two weeks, he'd tried to break up with Raven, but every time he'd bring up their relationship, she would lead the conversation in another direction. Almost as if she sensed where he was going. He didn't want to hurt her, but he felt so guilty. And there was the complication that Raven was Iris' goddaughter, the only child of her best friend, Ellie. If he broke up with Raven, Iris and Luc might feel caught in the middle of an unwelcome drama. But he had a right to live his own life, didn't he?

Yet now, Luna was gone. He needed help to find her, and Iris was the only one he knew with any experience tracking people down. It wasn't her profession, but she was good at it. He didn't want to have to explain his true feelings to Iris and his father, but after Luna's phone call, that was the least of his worries.

CHAPTER 10
SOUR PLUM DUCK

Back home in Cambridge, Iris sat in front of a blazing fire, her slippered feet up on an ottoman, a cup of hot cider warming her hands. She tried to make sense of the information she'd received that day.

"Dinner will be ready in a few minutes," Luc called from their large, open-plan kitchen.

Iris took a last sip of her drink. "What are you making?"

"You'll see." Since Luc's restaurant was open Tuesday through Saturday, by unspoken agreement, Iris cooked most Sunday nights and Luc experimented with new recipes on Mondays.

The cooking aroma from the kitchen was savory, redolent of caramelized onions and other mysteries.

Iris studied Luc's back as he stirred something in a pan on the stove and paused to taste it from a wooden spoon. She couldn't get out of her head what he'd said on their vacation the previous month, that he was having trouble living with her given her constant involvement in dangerous situations. For Luc, it brought back the anxiety of growing up with a policeman father, who was eventually killed on the job.

And to think that Iris had been expecting him to propose that evening! She felt mortified even thinking about it now.

The next day, Luc had backpedaled from his words, assuring Iris that they'd be able to make their life together work. Had he scared himself? Regardless, doubt had crept in. She didn't want to lose the life she had now, her life with Luc. And looking into Luna's disappearance for Ash might send her into dangerous waters.

Iris got up from her chair just as Luc came in, carrying a platter to the dining room table. She could identify some kind of poultry surrounded by a wreath of fresh scallions. "Can I do anything to help?"

"Why don't you pour us some of the Pinot Noir on the counter there."

"It's duck, right?"

"Sour plum duck. I'm experimenting with a recipe for Chinese New Year."

Not long after, they sat down for a feast. Iris thought it was perfect from start to finish, but Luc did his usual deconstructing of all the ingredients, typing into his iPad things he wanted to tweak. Such was life with a serious chef.

After their meal, Luc leaned back in his chair. "Did you learn anything helpful about the missing woman this afternoon?"

Iris filled him in on the information she'd been able to dig up: how an older woman had brought the boy to a studio near Luna's place to get them both passport photos and the photographer had comped them a contact sheet of the boy. One of those shots ended up in Luna's wallet. And on Friday afternoon, her neighbor had witnessed a man luring Luna into his car, a particular model of an Audi.

Luc tipped his head to the side as he listened to the descriptions.

"Sounds like this older woman and the kid were planning a trip." He held his fork in the air. "I wonder if the Audi guy is someone Luna was involved with, and they were just having a fight. She could have gone off with him to continue the argument, then they made up and spent a long weekend together."

Iris shook her head. "If that were the case, she would have gone back to lock up her studio and retrieve the cat. Luna also planned to meet Ash for dinner but then didn't show. She never called him to explain where she had gone."

"You said the neighbor thought he saw someone in the back seat of the car?"

"Yeah. I'm thinking it could have been the boy. If the man who knocked on Luna's window was holding the boy as a hostage, that could account for Luna running frantically out of her apartment. Whatever their relationship is, that little boy is important to her."

"Maybe." Luc stacked the dinner plates. "That model Audi is pretty high-end. I wonder how many are sold around here. Not a lot, I'd guess. It's lucky that graphic designer knows his car models. Maybe Ed can track it down."

"Speaking of Ed, how did you two make out looking for the uncle?"

"Turns out there's only one Frank Esposito living in Revere, and he's eight years old. Luna gave a fake reference, taking the chance Ash wouldn't follow up. Anyway, we drove out to the address she'd listed in Revere as her former residence. We showed Luna's picture to the people there and around the neighborhood, but no one recognized her." Luc turned on the espresso machine. "Ed called a contact at the DMV to search for a copy of her driver's license, but there's nothing on file in Massachusetts, at least not under Luna Esposito. Ed thinks, given the lack of ID and the false address, that Luna Esposito may not be her real name."

As Iris and Luc cleared the table, another thought occurred to her. "I couldn't find any place within walking distance of the studio where Luna might have worked. I wonder how she got money to pay her rent, buy food, and cover her painting supplies?" Iris loaded the dishwasher, then straightened up. "I suppose she could have taken a bus to a job further away."

"You just looked at service jobs—cleaning houses, bartending, waitressing, right?" Luc asked.

"Ash said she was in her studio most days, painting. So, she couldn't have had a nine-to-five job. And whatever she did, she must have been getting paid under the table if she was trying to stay off the grid."

Luc brought a pair of decaf espressos to the dining room, and they sat back down. "She could have a job that allows working from home, telecommuting or taking meetings over Zoom. Something part-time."

"How do we find out about that?"

"Did you see any mail addressed to her in the studio? Any laptops?"

"No computer. I just found drawing stuff in her desk. It's like this woman doesn't exist. How are we supposed to find a ghost?"

"Hey—we're not professionals. We shouldn't even be doing this," Luc said.

"I was thinking the same thing. Why don't we tell Ash what we've learned and let him take it from here?" Iris didn't want to give Luc any reason to think that *she* was the one pushing to get involved with the artist's disappearance. "Given the neighbor who witnessed Luna's departure on Friday, maybe the police will take an interest in tracking down the Audi. Then again, the cops might think Jess' story proves Luna left of her own accord and isn't really missing."

Luc checked the time on his phone. "It's only seven. Let's call Ash."

CHAPTER 11
A GHOST WITH A CAT

The next time the phone rang, as Ash was reheating a bowl of Thai coconut soup, he grabbed for his mobile and answered without checking caller ID. "Luna?"

"No, it's Luc... What? Did Luna contact you?"

"Yeah, ten minutes ago. I was hoping she'd call back."

"I'm putting you on speakerphone. Iris is here."

Ash described the call.

"Wow," Iris said. "Was there any way you could tell where she was calling from? Any background noise or other voices?"

"No. I listened hard, but the call was too quick. It sounded like someone grabbed the phone away from her. Did you find out anything today?"

Iris filled him in on their discoveries, including what Luc's father's police partner had told him. "Ed thinks she might be using a fake identity."

This floored Ash. "Why would she do that?"

"She could be hiding from someone," Luc said. "Your other tenant, Jess, saw a man in an Audi knock on her window before she ran outside screaming. Did she ever mention any guy harassing her?"

"No. Jess saw that? The guy must be who has her now. He must have kidnapped her!"

"But it sounds like she ran out to meet him willingly."

Ash stayed silent, considering what this meant.

Iris interrupted his thoughts. "How did Luna learn about the studio for rent?"

"I put up a notice in a few coffeeshops around here for a live-work space for artists. They had to show me their portfolios or websites to make sure they were legit and not just scamming for a cheap place to live."

"Do you remember anything from her website or rental form that might give us more information about her?" Luc asked. "Her web address, for example, or art classes she might have taken?"

"Luna said she'd been living with an uncle in Revere since her parents died, and she showed me scans of her paintings. We already had someone who builds mixed-media constructions and a graphic designer living here, so I liked the thought of another painter."

"You said she paid her rent in cash." Iris said. "But she never indicated how she got money?"

"Like I said, I just figured she had a waitressing job at night and was getting paid off the books."

"I showed her picture around a lot of restaurants and bars in your area today," Iris said. "No one recognized her. Did she ever mention any places she liked to hang out?"

"We'd go to the Healthy Planet sometimes, but I don't remember her mentioning any other places, or even other people in her life."

A feeling of futility swept over Ash. "How are we going to find her? Luna wants my help, but she hasn't left me any path to follow. And now she's vanished into the ether."

"Not completely," Iris said. "She left the cat. Maybe it has a microchip."

"Hey yeah." Ash glanced down at Kevin, who was licking a paw. "How do I find out about that?"

"Take him to a vet. They can scan him to check," Iris said.

There was a pause before Luc added, "See if that turns up anything, but I think it's time to contact the police again. Especially after that phone call you got. Maybe Ed can call someone he knows on the Medford Police force and convince them to start a missing person search. We've taken this as far as we can ourselves."

CHAPTER 12
THE RESCUE LEAGUE

Early the next morning, Ash went to the front hall closet of his studio to retrieve a pair of thick leather gloves from the pocket of his coat. The damned cat had already left several bloody scratches on his hands. He cursed as he slipped on the gloves and wrapped an old sweatshirt around the squirming Kevin. He tied the shirt's arms in a knot in front, so Kevin, howling, appeared to be in a straitjacket.

"Any more lip from you and you're getting a gag." Ash had looked through Luna's studio earlier for a cat carrier, with no luck. God knew how she transported this devil spawn. Medford Veterinary Clinic was only a ten-minute drive away, most of which Ash spent tuning out the shirt-wrapped, seat-belted Kevin's outraged protests.

The receptionist lifted an eyebrow when Ash entered, holding his furious cat-burrito.

"I called earlier to get this cat checked for a microchip."

A scrub-clad technician soon appeared in the waiting room and warily took Kevin out of Ash's arms. "An unhappy customer," she noted.

"I'm hoping he's microchipped," Ash said, "so I can get his contact information. I want to get him back to his owner."

The tech returned five minutes later, cradling a now-subdued Kevin on Ash's rolled-up sweatshirt. "The chip gives his address as the Animal Rescue League of Boston. Whoever adopted him didn't update the information. But the League might have more records for him."

Ash thanked her and returned to the reception desk to pay for the visit. Once back at the car, he rewrapped and strapped the cat into the passenger seat and looked up the Animal Rescue League of Boston on his phone. It was about seven miles away in Boston's South End.

He steered his ancient station wagon onto Interstate Ninety-three South. The car shimmied as it accelerated over sixty. "Looks like I'm on my own trying to find your owner," he said to Kevin, who looked unimpressed. On the phone the previous night, it sounded like Iris and Luc were washing their hands of the search for Luna. He couldn't blame them. There were almost no leads, and they couldn't understand how much she meant to him.

Ash circled the block and swooped into a parking space another car had just vacated. Once he'd parked, Ash unwrapped the cat and carried him into the building.

The young volunteer in the red ARL shirt, whose name tag read *Stacy*, peered suspiciously at the overweight cat now sitting on the counter. "Is that Kevin? You aren't returning him, are you?"

"You recognize him?"

Kevin swiped at Stacy, lightly scratching her forearm. Ash quickly swaddled the cat in his sweatshirt again and confined the animal to the crook of his arm.

"Uh, Kevin was famous." Stacy examined her arm and frowned.

"We couldn't believe it when that lady...um, never mind. Can I help you?"

"Yeah. He got loose, and I'm trying to find his owner. Kevin's microchip only lists the Rescue League as his address."

"Really? We didn't add the adopter's contact info? That's weird."

"I just had a vet check it."

"Hmm." Stacy tapped on her keyboard. "I remember he was adopted right after Halloween. The woman who chose him said she liked a cat with spirit." Stacy snorted and rolled her eyes.

She scrolled down a list on her monitor. "Ah, I remember now. She gave her name, but said she was about to move, so didn't leave an address. Just a phone number."

"That's fine. If I can get that, I can get Kevin back to her."

"Sorry, I can't do that. We don't give out the name of the adopter."

He smiled, trying to turn on the charm. "Why not? I'm just trying to return someone's cat. What harm could that do?"

"I really wish I could help." Stacy sighed dramatically, then glared at Kevin. "I hope you don't want us to keep him. Normally we take our animals back, but we're full."

"That's okay. Kevin can stay with me," Ash assured her.

Stacy smiled. "Alright then. Good luck. I need to go wash this scratch before it gets infected."

Ash slow walked to the front door until she'd disappeared around a corner of the hall. Holding Kevin like a football, he raced back to her computer, took out his phone, and photographed the register. After scurrying back to the client side of the reception desk, he pinch-enlarged the screenshot. The November second line showed a name and phone number without an address. The adopter was Basia Sobieski. Just as Ash turned to leave, Stacy reappeared. She looked from him to her computer screen and raised an eyebrow.

"I don't know if this helps," she said, "but I carried Kevin to the adopter's car in a cardboard carrier. We always give them one of those with some cat food and a collar. I remember her car had a Beacon Hill resident sticker on it."

CHAPTER 13
A NEW COMMISSION

Iris was at her desk first thing on Tuesday morning. Loretta sat across from her, already going over requests from prospective new clients.

Loretta consulted her iPad. "I let Michael Barrett know you couldn't fit in his restaurant design in Back Bay this year."

"Or ever. We need more work, but Barrett wants a clone of Luc's restaurant, and I'm not doing that." *Unless we're really desperate and, even then, I'd make it look different.*

"Someone called yesterday asking if you'd design their new ice cream shop in Davis Square. Are you interested?"

"Just what Somerville needs: another ice cream store. Still, it could be a fun project for Rollo. Email me the details."

Loretta clacked some keys, then looked up and grinned. "I saved the best for last. We got an email from Jack and Anna Peterson, who own some property overlooking Wingaersheek Beach in Gloucester. They want to hire you to design a new house for them. They loved the house you did for Norman Meeker, which they saw in *cuttingedgedecor* and they've seen Lillian Butterworth's penthouse."

Iris sat up in her chair. "Now we're talking! Do we know them? Send me their email. Did you do any research on the land?"

"I'll send you the Google Earth link. It's beachfront, so there's a big setback from the high-water line. The Town doesn't list any other restrictions or liens on the property. Jack Peterson says he inherited it from his parents two years ago. He's the CEO of a company that makes educational toys, good ones. Anna oversees marketing for the firm. And before you ask, I checked. They're solvent."

Iris thought out loud: "I'll probably need to get our structural engineer to design a complicated foundation. Storm surge could have a big effect on what we can build."

"I take it we're accepting the job?"

"Let me read their letter and do some more research, but assuming they have a realistic budget, I can't imagine turning down this commission. We should schedule an in-person meeting." New construction was like catnip for architects, especially on a dynamite site with a view and for clients who already like your work.

"Have you spoken with Milo?" Loretta asked.

"I called him yesterday. He swears he'll have everything checked off on the museum punch list by the end of today. I'll do a walk-through tomorrow morning to make sure."

"Jason has the film crew scheduled to meet you and Alex Harcon at nine on Friday morning for the final taping."

"Yup, it's on my schedule."

"Okay, boss. I'll set up a meeting with the Petersons." Loretta left the office, humming to herself.

Iris carefully read the email from the prospective new clients. They sounded ideal, at least on paper. They complimented her previous projects but wanted to give her latitude to use her creative vision for them. Google Earth showed a generously sized lot for the area set on a high cliff. The project looked almost too perfect. Just as Iris was imagining all the possible hidden pitfalls, her phone buzzed and showed an unfamiliar caller ID. She picked up. "Hello?"

"Is this Iris Reid?" The man's quavering voice sounded vaguely familiar. "It's Sam Gilday from the photography studio in Medford."

"Oh, yes. Did you come across the woman with the boy again?"

"Unfortunately, yes. There was an article about a home invasion in the *Medford Chronicle* today. I recognized the person in the driver's license photo they showed as the woman who'd been in my studio. The paper said she'd been shot several days ago and discovered by the neighbors, who noticed a smell coming from her apartment."

"Did the article mention the boy?" Iris felt a chill running through her at the thought of him being in the apartment with the dead woman for several days.

Mr. Gilday continued. "The police said it was probably a robbery. Her name was Basia Sobieski, but there was no mention of the child."

CHAPTER 14
THE MEDFORD CHRONICLE

Iris did an internet search for Basia Sobieski. Besides the *Medford Chronicle* article, there was a brief write-up in *The Boston Globe*. She read both of them carefully and printed them out. What did this mean as far as Luna was concerned? The articles estimated Basia had died some time on Friday. No one had heard the shots. The apartment was ten minutes away from Luna's studio. Basia had brought the boy in for the two of them to get passport photos, and Luna carried a contact photo of him in her wallet. Could Basia's death be linked to Luna's disappearance?

And what was the woman's relationship to the boy who seemed to be important to Luna; was he a relative? Had the child been living with Basia?

The night before, Iris and Luc had urged Ash to let the police take over the search for Luna. But without knowing about Basia's connection to Luna through the boy, the police were attributing her death to a random home invasion. How could they discover the link without the information Iris had found? And where was the boy now? If Basia had been murdered and the child kidnapped, then this entire case had just gotten a lot more dangerous. Iris needed to discuss this with Luc.

Luc's schedule was non-stop from Tuesday morning until after the restaurant's last service on Saturday night, but there was always a lull after his early morning shopping at the food markets and before the intense afternoon prep with his team got underway.

She leaned back in her office chair and pressed his number on speed dial. Luc answered right away. "Hey babe. What's up?"

She filled him in on the death of Basia Sobieski and how the woman might fit into the puzzle of Luna's disappearance.

"And there's a chance the little boy was kidnapped?" Luc asked.

"If he was living with Basia, somebody might have used him to lure Luna into that car on Friday. Maybe Basia was collateral damage."

The police need to know about this. Let me call Ed. Maybe he can go down to the station with Ash to lend more weight to the case."

"Wait. Given what the Medford police put Ash through last year, trying to railroad him for murder, do you think they might suspect Ash of being behind this Luna business?"

"Even though *he's* the one who's been trying to get them to take her disappearance seriously?" Luc paused. "But you might be right. Would you have time to go down there with Ed and Ash to fill the police in on the finer points of these connections and give Ash some insulation from their suspicions? I wish I could go too, but Arnold called in sick tonight, and I don't have cover."

Iris checked her watch. "I need to get some lunch now, but I can head over to the station with them this afternoon. Why don't you call Ash and Ed? Fill them in on the latest news and call me back with a time."

She spent the next twenty minutes at Rollo's desk going over his

Brewster Street shop drawings, then collected his and Loretta's lunch orders. The Hi-Rise Bakery made the best sandwiches in the area. By the time Iris made it through the long line and returned with three bulging bags, her phone was buzzing. She handed Loretta her lunch and slipped the phone out of her pocket.

Luc's voice on the line sounded excited. "You're not going to believe what Ash just learned. Basia Sobieski was the one who adopted Kevin, Luna's damned cat."

CHAPTER 15
MEETING THE DETECTIVE

At a little after two that afternoon, Iris pulled up in front of Ed Rostow's triple-decker in Inman Square. He'd gained a lot of weight in retirement, and when he maneuvered himself into the car, he filled the passenger seat. Ed greeted her warmly and leaned over to give her an awkward side-hug.

He was a smart and kind man, but Iris worried that the gin-blossoms on his cheeks were more pronounced than the last time she'd seen him. Should Luc try to talk with him about his drinking? It wasn't their place to interfere. At least she didn't smell fresh alcohol on him.

"I've made us an appointment with a friend from the Cambridge PD who transferred to Medford when his family moved there." Ed pulled the seat belt out all the way and managed to wrap it across himself. "Name is David Stroud. We want to keep this case away from Detective Gonzalez, the guy who was gunning for Ash last year."

"Oh, I remember Gonzalez," Iris said.

"You'll like David," Ed assured her. "Luc filled me in on the details but, before we pick up Ash, I'm curious about something. This Luna woman called Ash and asked for his help, right? What's their relationship? Friends or more than friends?"

"Good question. I'd like to know that myself since he's been seeing my goddaughter pretty seriously for the last eighteen months."

"I remember her from the hospital after Ash got shot. Sweet kid with a weird name."

"Raven."

"Yeah, right. So, you think Ash might have developed feelings for this tenant of his?"

"I don't know. They're both painters, and Luna is beautiful. Maybe Ash will open up more with us today. But he'd better not break Raven's heart."

Iris navigated through the streets and unpredictable crosswalks around Tufts University and arrived ten minutes later in front of Ash's building.

Ash must have been watching for them because he immediately jogged out to the car, crawling into the back. "Hey, Ed. Good to see you, man." They shook hands through the opening between the front seats. "Thank you both for setting this up and coming along with me."

"I'm hoping my buddy, David Stroud, can open a missing person case file and use the information you've collected to find this woman."

"God, I hope so. Luna sounded completely terrified on the phone."

"You haven't heard from her since then, have you?" Iris asked.

"No, and that worries me," Ash said. "It feels like she's being held captive somewhere."

When they arrived at the three-story brick police station, Iris heard Ash suck in a breath. *He's got to have bad memories of this place from being grilled by Gonzalez last year.*

They checked in at the reception desk with a young, uniformed officer. He directed them to wait in the row of fiberglass chairs lining the hallway. Ed chose to stand.

At two-thirty, a tall Black man in a sports jacket got off the elevator and approached them. He carried himself with the confidence of a seasoned detective and reached out a hand to Ed. "Detective Rostow, you just can't stay away from a precinct house, can you?"

Iris noticed Ash's shoulders relax at the sight of a Black detective.

Ed smiled. "David, good to see you again. You remember Scott Cormier and his son Luc? This is Luc's partner, Iris Reid, and his son, Ashley Burke." They shook hands, and David led them all to a first-floor conference room.

The four of them took seats around a battered wooden table. A single small window overlooked the parking lot. The room was chilly, and Iris kept her parka zipped up.

"I'm going to record our talk to make sure I get all the details right." Stroud laid his phone on the table. "That okay with all of you?"

They agreed, so Stroud recited the date and people present. "Now, I understand from Ed that you, Ash, were here last Friday and tried to file a missing-person case for a Luna Esposito. She's a friend and a tenant in a building you own. You were told that there was not enough evidence at the time to categorize her as missing. But it's now been five days." He tapped his fingers on the table, looking at Ash. "And you haven't heard anything from Ms. Esposito since she left?"

"Yes. She called last night, and we got cut off." Ash described the brief conversation.

Iris thought she noted a look of alarm in the detective's eyes before he continued. "Ed says you've also discovered a link between Ms. Esposito and Basia Sobieski, who was found deceased at the end of last week."

"Actually, two links." Ash leaned forward as he went through the steps, from finding the picture of the boy, to its photographer recognizing Basia as the woman who'd come with the child to his studio for passport photos.

Stroud stopped the recording. "That would explain the toys and child's clothes found in Ms. Sobieski's apartment. A connection to a missing child escalates this case." He pressed the record button again. "Other than finding a photo of this boy in Ms. Esposito's wallet, do you know how the boy is related to her?"

"No, although it was the only photo we found of anyone in Luna's studio. She paid for everything in cash and had no ID in her wallet, so it seems like she was living off the grid, maybe hiding from someone." Ash said. "For her to take the risk of keeping this photo, the boy must mean a lot to her."

Stroud grunted in agreement. "You said there was a second link?"

"Yes, Luna left her cat behind when she ran out of the building—"

"Wait," Stroud said. "Did anyone see her leaving the building?"

"Yes, I'll get back to that but let me finish telling you that Luna's cat was microchipped with the name of the Boston Animal Rescue League. Their records show that the woman who originally adopted Luna's cat was Basia Sobieski. She didn't give her address because she said she was about to move, but her car had a Beacon Hill resident sticker on it."

"You're quite the detective, Ashley. Your grandfather would be proud of you," Stroud said.

"Iris and Ed helped," Ash said. "In fact, Iris, you should describe what Jess saw when Luna left on Friday."

So, Iris did. Stroud interrupted twice to get contact names and details about the car. Then he was silent for a few moments. "This certainly casts Ms. Sobieski's death in a different light."

After being assured that he now had all the details, the detective ended the recording. "I'd say we have more than enough to start a missing person case for your friend, but our best hope of finding her is knowing everything we can about Luna Esposito. We need to build a victim profile. Her connection to the dead woman and a missing child raises this case to high priority."

CHAPTER 16
LUNA-FRIDAY

L una raced out the building's door toward the car. She could see Paul's scared little face in the back window. He was crying.

"No-oo-oo!" she screamed. She grabbed hold of the rear door latch and, miraculously, it opened. An unfamiliar woman sitting on the far side of the back seat pulled Paul away from her.

"Mommy!" he cried, wriggling his arms free and reaching out frantically toward her.

"Let him go, Helen," Goran yelled from the driver's seat. Luna could see Malik's henchman watching her in the rearview mirror as she climbed in next to her son. The door locks clicked shut. "It may be the last time the kid sees his mama unless she starts to cooperate."

Luna gripped Paul on her lap, stroking his hair, whispering, "It's going to be alright. Mommy's here. We'll be fine." She knew neither of them believed it.

Where was Basia? Luna felt sick at the thought Goran might

have injured or even killed her friend when he came for Paul. Had her son witnessed some awful violence? How had Malik tracked them down?

She stared out the window as the car accelerated hard onto Interstate Ninety-three South, the main artery leading into Boston. Luna's plan had failed, and now she and her son would be prisoners again. What was this cycle of captivity and separation doing to him?

Malik had imprisoned them six months ago, keeping Paul from her for all but short visits. It had been agony. If Luna hadn't learned that Basia, the nanny Malik hired, was kind to the toddler in her charge, she wouldn't have been able to go on with her life. Being kept apart from Paul ate away at her, and she knew it was affecting him, too.

But then, three months ago, with Basia's help, Luna had engineered their escape.

They should have run farther. But the only contact Luna had to get them new identity papers was through an art school friend in Boston's South End. She figured Malik would never look for her in Medford, thirty minutes away yet a world apart from his tony Beacon Hill life. And having Paul live with Basia, now loyal to Luna, and staying in a separate apartment, would muddy the trail more. Meanwhile, Luna could quietly visit Paul in the mornings and spend her afternoons and evenings painting. She'd had to use some of the savings from her father, cash she'd stashed in a bank safe deposit box as soon as she first got to Boston. But the sale of her "Prisoner" series under an assumed name would provide income in their new location and supply the reward she had promised Basia for her help. Where had her plan gone wrong?

When Goran pulled the Audi into the private parking space in front of Malik's Louisburg Square townhouse, Helen wrenched

Paul back from Luna's arms and carried the boy up the steps into the house.

As her son was being propelled into a room on the third floor, Luna called out to him. "Be a good boy, Paul. I'll see you soon. I love you, baby." Goran dragged her by the elbow up another flight of stairs to her old attic studio.

LUNA SAT ON THE FLOOR SHIVERING. SHE KNEW EVERY CORNER OF THE drafty room by heart. Why hadn't she grabbed her coat on the way out of Ash's building? After three months in this prison the last time, she'd been lucky to escape with Paul. Malik would never hire another nanny who could be persuaded to switch loyalties. Could she ever devise a second way out?

During her two years studying at the Art Academy of Boston, she'd visited Beacon Hill a number of times. Its brick row houses, and gas streetlights had seemed charming at the time. The most affluent section was Louisburg Square. She had admired the bow-fronted townhouses surrounding a small, oval-shaped park.

Now she was a captive again in one of those homes, and her only interest in its architecture was in figuring out how to escape from it. The fact of the houses being built shoulder-to-shoulder meant that if she could climb up to the roof, somehow carrying Paul with her, maybe she could scramble over to a neighboring house.

But she'd already thought through the limitations of that plan. Her attic door was always locked, and the room had no windows. The only light came from three large skylights, letting in diffuse north light. But even if she could move the heavy bureau under one of them and climb up on top of it, the skylights didn't open. She'd checked. And she knew it was impossible to break through the plexiglass.

She heard the floorboards on the stairs squeak. Someone turned a key in her door's lock to open it.

CHAPTER 17
AN APPOINTMENT

After Iris dropped Ed off back home, she voice-activated a call to Loretta as she drove. "Hi, it's me. Any fires you need put out?"

"All under control, boss. I set up an appointment for the Petersons to meet with you on Thursday at noon. I figured I could put out sandwiches and pastries in the conference room. That sound okay?"

"Perfect. Did you confirm a time with Milo for me to do the museum walk-through?"

"He asked you to meet him tomorrow morning at the site at nine. He wants you to bring him a cup of that tea he likes from Simon's."

Iris laughed. "So now I'm his gofer?" Simon's was the coffee shop next door to Iris' loft. She and her contractor Milo had become friends through their many projects together.

When Iris got home, after an obligatory few minutes rubbing Sheba's tummy and throwing her stuffed hedgehog to be fetched, she turned on the espresso machine and made herself a decaf latte.

It was four o'clock, and here she was, playing with her dog and lounging on the sofa. Shouldn't she be hustling up more projects for her firm? Hiring some more architects? But she'd already produced the gold-standard in architectural commissions—a museum. A small one, but she'd packed a lot of innovative design into it. The Peterson job sounded like another plum.

Other than some wobbly issues with Luc, her life felt comfortable now. But if there was one thing she'd learned in life, it was times like this when all of a sudden everything went to hell.

The rude buzz of her phone interrupted her thoughts. Ash's name showed up on the caller ID.

"Hi, Ash. What's up?"

"I just remembered something. Luna mentioned she'd gone to the Art Academy in Boston. What if she used her real name there? We could show her picture around to the instructors, and some students might remember her. That could give us clues about her background. They might even know about some bad actor who might have been hassling her."

"Wait—I thought you were going to leave the search to Detective Stroud. We just gave him all our background information. He can use police resources to dig much deeper than we can."

"The people at the academy might not be into talking to cops. They could think Luna's in some kind of trouble and not want to rat her out. If you and I went together, they wouldn't see me as some stalker ex-boyfriend she was trying to get away from. Detective Stroud said we needed a victim profile."

Damn. Ash was not going to let this go. What was the hold this woman had over him?

"Okay," Iris said. "I have something to do tomorrow at nine. Meet me here at ten-thirty and we can see if this leads anywhere."

CHAPTER 18
OLYMPIA REDUX

On Wednesday morning during her walk-through of the museum, Iris checked off all the items on the punch list. Milo assured her that professional cleaners would burnish all three levels to glow for Friday's final video production.

They stood in the tall atrium, admiring the sculptural effect of the overhanging balconies.

Milo pointed with his chin. "The green wall of plants looks awesome."

"Mmm," Iris answered. She hated that the idea for it had come from her former intern, Roger, who had infiltrated her office under false pretenses. "On this last taping, do you want to say something about your crew or the construction process?"

Milo grinned. "Like how the project's success owes everything to the brilliant architect's design?"

"That's understood, but maybe something that would bring you more work. This film is a marketing opportunity for both of us."

He pulled the elastic out of his long ponytail and shook out his hair. "Oh, right. I'll try to think of something by then."

71

Iris checked her phone. "I've gotta run. See you Friday."

She jogged the half mile from Harvard Square up Mass Ave and was perspiring under her parka by the time she reached home. Ash stood waiting beside his station wagon in the restaurant's parking lot.

"Am I early?" he asked.

"No, I'm ready. The Academy is right across from the MFA, isn't it?"

"Yup. I guess you can park in the museum lot if there are no spaces on the street."

They got into her car as Iris considered. Parking was always a major hassle in any part of Boston, but Wednesday mid-morning might not be too bad. The trip across the Charles River, along Storrow Drive and around the Fenway took them twenty minutes. Finding a parking space four blocks away took another twenty.

The Boston Art Academy was a four-story brick warehouse with huge industrial windows, admitting great natural light and, no doubt, winter cold.

"This place is a lot bigger than our entire art department at UMass," Ash said.

Outside the entrance, Iris stopped. "Have you figured out an approach? The registrar may not be willing to give out information about former students."

"Follow me," Ash said.

A bored-looking guard sitting behind a front desk stopped them. "ID please."

Ash whipped out his UMass student ID, which had technically expired the previous June on his graduation. He said, "Professor Linsky told me to check out the alumni show upstairs." He tipped his head toward Iris. "She's my mother, visiting."

Iris tried to keep a straight face. The guard waved them in, and they headed for the stairs.

"What's the plan, *son*?" Was she really old enough to have a twenty-one-year-old son? Her seven-years-younger boyfriend actually was Ash's parent, so yes, she really was that old. Yikes.

Ash fished the picture of Luna out of his wallet. "I figured we'd wander around and ask people if they recognize her."

Iris didn't comment on how scattershot she thought that strategy was.

In the hallway, several artsy student-types dismissively shook their heads at the image. Ash approached an older woman who looked to be an instructor. She was around Iris' age, mid-forties, and her dirty blond hair was spilling out from a messy bun. She lowered the reading glasses from atop her head and peered intently at the photo. Her left eye twitched noticeably before she handed the photo back. "No, she doesn't look familiar. Sorry." She hurried away.

By now, they had reached a spacious room with glass windows and a door revealing large and small artwork hanging on the walls. Sculptures and multimedia constructions sat on pedestals in the middle of the space. Iris followed Ash inside. A sign near the entry indicated that this was a permanent exhibit of student art.

Iris regarded Ash. "How did you know this was here?"

"Luna told me the school had kept one of her paintings for this show. She regretted giving it to them because it was one of her favorites."

Ash led them in a clockwise direction, moving quickly from piece to piece. Three-quarters of the way around the room, he stopped before a large, unframed canvas. Even Iris recognized it as Luna's style. The oil painting realistically depicted Édouard Manet's nude Olympia, wearing a flower in her hair and not much else. But instead of being sprawled on a bed and attended by a servant, she was lounging on a rubber mat with a yoga class going on around her, very much a scene from the present day.

73

Ash laughed. "You gotta love Luna's sense of humor."

They checked the little white card below the painting. It read, "Olympia Redux." The artist's name was Celia Núñez.

Ash scratched the back of his neck. "Is that Luna's real name? She doesn't seem like a Celia."

"That still may not be the name on her birth certificate," Iris pointed out. "But there could be information about her attached to that identity."

They continued around the room to confirm they had correctly picked out Luna's work and retreated to the hall just as a classroom was emptying. They watched the crowd, then Ash went up to a young man with bushy eyebrows who looked slightly older than the others and offered Luna's photo.

"Hey man, can you tell me if this is Celia Núñez? She studied here last year, I think."

The man stepped back and looked at Ash suspiciously. "Why do you want to know?"

A woman with a mermaid tattoo running down her neck and disappearing beneath her sweater stepped in and grabbed the photo. "You're asking about Cele? Do you know where she is?" She squinted at the picture. "Is this what she looks like now? She's lost a ton of weight and grown out the blue tips in her hair. But that's the necklace with the Athena coin she always wore. Yeah, those are her features." She looked up quickly at Ash. "Where is she? Is the baby okay?"

Iris and Ash exchanged looks. He answered, "She was living in my studio building in Medford, but there was no baby with her. She disappeared last week. Then I got a brief phone call from her asking for help, but she got cut off before she could say where she was. I'm really worried."

"Join the club," Bushy Eyebrows said. "She disappeared off the face of the earth last summer. It wasn't like her to bail on her friends."

Iris joined the conversation. "She's been calling herself Luna Esposito and living off the grid, paying for everything with cash. We think she's been hiding out from someone and we're afraid that person's caught up with her. If you can tell us more about her, maybe we can figure out where she is now."

"Bloody hell! Poor Cele." Mermaid Tattoo was about to say more, but Bushy Eyebrows put a hand on her arm and said to Ash, "How can we be sure you're not the ones she's hiding from?"

Ash took out his phone and scrolled through his photos. He held it out so they could see the screen. "My name's Ashley Burke, and I'm a painter too. This is a larger shot of Lu...I mean Cele in my studio with one of my paintings. Does she look scared of me?"

The two art students peered at his screen. "I guess not," the woman conceded.

Ash swiped through his pictures again and showed them another one. "And she had this photo of a young boy in the wallet she left behind."

When Mermaid Tattoo saw it, she gasped. "It's Paul! Look how big he's gotten. But he looks sad."

Bushy Eyebrows looked around the now-empty hallway. "Let's find somewhere more private. We should talk."

CHAPTER 19

LUNA-FRIDAY

That evening, an elderly woman with downcast eyes set a dinner tray onto the floor just inside Luna's room.

"Please help me! I'm being held prisoner," Luna cried out.

The woman looked up, alarmed. "No English." She quickly backed out of the room and locked the door.

Luna stared down at the dinner of chicken, rice, and peas on a paper plate along with plastic utensils. Nothing she could use as a weapon.

After a while, the door opened again. Goran dragged her tray with its uneaten meal into the hall and returned. "Get up. He wants to see you."

Goran escorted Luna downstairs to a sumptuous living room and shoved her into an armchair facing Malik, who sat in front of a blaze burning in the fireplace. Goran remained in the room, guarding the doorway.

Malik looked just as Luna remembered—silver hair slicked back, aristocratic features set in an imperious expression. Every bit the urbane art appraiser his clients expected. He wore a burgundy cashmere sweater over gray flannel pants and regarded Luna over tortoiseshell glasses.

He had visited the Art Academy as a guest critic a year ago, when Luna was taking Audrey Glenn's course on nineteenth-century oil painting techniques. She had been experimenting with combining that style with her customary modern approach. Malik had immediately zeroed in on Luna's work. Her skill in painting people realistically had always been exceptional. He was captivated by her *Olympia Redux*.

Malik took a sip of the gold liquid, the dancing flames from the fireplace reflected in the cut glass crystal. He set the snifter down carefully on an antique side table. "Welcome back, Celia. Or should I call you Luna now? Or maybe you'd prefer 'Il Fantasma's daughter?'"

Luna's skin was finally warm, but her insides turned to ice. "The Ghost." She hadn't heard that name in a long time.

"After you disappeared on me, I did a little research," Malik continued. "Some of my associates reminded me that the most talented but elusive forger of the last fifty years was rumored to have a daughter. Word was, she was almost as talented as he was. But the forger got himself killed two or three years ago, and his daughter disappeared. Marco Petrucci of the Providence crime family has been searching for this young woman ever since."

She tried not to shudder. "And you think I'm her? Because I can paint, and you've had me forge a painting for you?" Luna forced an unconvincing laugh. "That's quite a stretch."

"When you ran away from this townhouse, I wondered if you'd turn me in. Of course, I had safeguards in place for that possibility. But you didn't. Perhaps you couldn't afford to draw attention to yourself or to your various identities. My guess is you were hiding from the Petrucci family, not just from me."

Luna tried to keep her voice steady. "Did you share this far-fetched theory with your criminal friends?"

"And have them scoop you up when I need you here working for me?"

"Maybe I didn't want to get tangled up with the police, having to prove I knew nothing about your scams." Luna sat up in her chair. "Look, I did what you wanted. I copied the Renoir, and I'm sure you did very well switching it for the original. Now let Paul and me go. I won't say anything to the police. I've proven my discretion over the last few months."

"Oh, no. You're a valuable asset, Celia. You have a gift. We can't let that go to waste. You and your son will remain here as my guests until I decide otherwise."

"You can't keep us as prisoners. Think of Paul!" Luna tried to hold back tears. "He's an innocent child. He needs to be with his mother, not locked in a room with a jailer."

Malik slammed his glass on the table, spilling several drops on the wood. "Pull yourself together. We don't have time to waste on drama. It's time for your next assignment, and I hope you're up for a challenge. You can make your father proud."

Now she did break down, sobbing into her hands.

"Pay attention!" Malik shouted. "I have a new painting for you to copy, and I'm only going to give you these instructions once. The client is traveling in Europe, so I was given twelve days to perform my appraisal tests. We've already used up four of those days."

Luna sat up rigidly and wiped the tears from her cheeks.

"You will strip down the vintage canvas I've provided and copy the masterpiece onto it. After completing your version, you'll need to perform all the historic layers of glazing. We'll use the oven again, like we did for the Renoir, to create the crackling effect. I will set up a precise schedule. If you make enough daily progress, you will be allowed to spend an hour each afternoon with Paul. Under

Helen's supervision, of course. And don't even think about trying to win her sympathy. I assure you, she's no Basia."

Luna pushed her fear about Basia's fate to the back of her mind and tried to focus on Paul's and her own. A large, shrouded mound stood behind Malik's chair—a cloth covering something propped on a stand. Despite her despair, Luna couldn't help feeling a sliver of curiosity about which new masterpiece she would experience up close this time.

"Goran is outfitting your room with a few books about the artist along with exact matches of the brushes and paints the artist would have used. We will also supply you with some clothes and blankets for your stay. If you need any more supplies, leave a note when your dishes are collected after meals. Now, are you ready to see your new project?"

Malik rose from his chair and stood next to the easel. He dramatically whipped the canvas cover off the painting.

Seeing it, Luna could barely breathe. She was terrified.

After a few moments of shocked silence, she whispered, "No, I can't copy that! I'm not good enough. No one is."

"You'd better hope you are. For Paul's sake. Besides, I may tell the collector that it's a fake. A very good forgery that the gallery is trying to pass off as an original. The gallery will think they were swindled by whomever they bought it from."

Luna stood before the John Singer Sargent portrait of a boy. She had never seen this specific painting. It was one of the lesser known of the eight hundred portraits the Master had produced. But his style was unmistakable. And over the next eight days, she would live with it, studying every detail and trying to replicate its magic.

If she failed, the stakes were too high to imagine.

CHAPTER 20
LUNA-SATURDAY

The next morning at dawn, Luna lay on a thin mattress on the floor of her garret. Her lips formed words, but no sound escaped.

Papa, I've failed you. I tried to create a new life here in Boston with the money and new identity you left for me, but I drew attention to myself. I showed off by painting Olympia Redux, and now your grandson and I are prisoners. No one but Marco Petrucci ever knew your real identity. Now, this stronzo has traced me to you through my own stupid moves. And my poor sweet Paul suffers because of it.

She stared up at the clouds visible through the grimy skylights, her vision blurred from tears. Inside her head, she could hear her father's powerful voice.

Buy time until we work out a new plan. I'll help you and Paul like I did before. You will have your new life, but you must start on the painting and make the stronzo think he has won.

Luna dragged herself to her feet and studied the Sargent painting set on an easel. It showed a boy of about Paul's age holding a toy sailboat in a full-length pose. The boy shared Paul's dark coloring and melancholy expression. Was Malik taunting her? Children had been a typical subject for John Singer Sargent. This example was rendered in his early classical style, with vibrant light shown in strong contrast. The boy's face was luminous, and the painting's colors and effortless detail were stunning. How could she ever capture this level of virtuosity?

You can do it, her father assured her. I will guide you. It will be our capolavoro, our masterpiece.

Luna spent the rest of the morning studying the book Malik had provided about Sargent's particular technique while closely examining the brushwork on the painting she was to copy. Sargent painted wet-on-wet, meaning that fresh paint was applied without waiting for the underlayer of paint to dry thoroughly, a style he had learned from the French Impressionists. It required a lot of experience to lay in the color precisely, but luckily, Luna's father had schooled her in the procedure.

When Luna's lunch tray arrived, she forced herself to eat. She'd need to keep her mind and body strong. With the tray retrieval, Luna sent back a list of the supplies she needed: red sable Filbert brushes in varying widths, and a dozen tubes of historically and chemically accurate paint colors which she specified. She informed Malik that, crucially, he needed to provide a commercial oven with an interior large enough to fit the canvas for its multiple drying sessions.

She had learned from Audrey Glenn's class in art school that by baking a canvas repeatedly between layers of varnish for ninety-five minutes at 248 degrees Fahrenheit, she'd be able to produce a surface as hard and dry as a painting over one hundred years old. The earlier Renoir she had copied for him had been small enough to bake in his kitchen oven. But with this larger canvas, she'd need a larger oven, and she doubted Malik would have the heavy appliance hauled all the way up to her attic studio. More likely, it would be delivered and parked on a lower floor of the townhouse. While using it, she might have opportunities to escape. The trick would be finding a way to have Paul with her at that time.

Luna began the laborious process of stripping a third-rate landscape from the canvas that Malik had provided. It would have the same period-appropriate sizing and tacks as the real Sargent painting in order to pass the carbon-dating test. She would need to remove all the old paint carefully, because any image that remained under her new portrait would show up on an x-ray. Luna used acetone and turpentine, changing the cotton wool cloths frequently to keep the canvas clean. The old sizing was yellowed and needed a gentle bleaching. This tedious job took her until the early afternoon, by which time her back was killing her.

When Malik showed up, Luna felt woozy from the fumes coming off the used cloths piled inside a metal wastebasket.

"I'm going to pass out!" she said. "There's no ventilation in here."

"You managed just fine last time," he said, handing the wastebasket to Goran to put in the hall. "The canvas is stripped now. Stop complaining."

"I need to go outside. I feel sick, and I'm going to mess up the painting if I can't think straight."

Malik sighed heavily. After a moment, he said, "You may take a break now with your son. In his room. For one hour."

"I have to breathe fresh air. Let Paul and me walk outside around the square at least. Goran and Helen will be there. I'm sure they won't let us off the leash."

Malik shrugged and looked at Goran. "Fine. Give them half an hour out front. Shoot the kid if she tries anything."

IN PAUL'S ROOM, LUNA HUGGED HER SON TIGHTLY AS GORAN PASSED along the instructions to Helen.

"Is the lady being nice to you?" Luna whispered in Paul's ear.

But the small boy couldn't stop crying long enough to respond.

"We're going outside for a walk now," Luna told him.

"Can we go home and see Nana?" Paul asked.

This was his name for Basia. Did that mean her son hadn't witnessed anything bad happening to his nanny? Luna could only hope that was true. "We need to stay in this house for a little while. Then we can leave, okay?"

"But I don't like it here."

"I know, Paul. I'm sorry."

Once outside, Luna took a deep breath of chilly air, trying to expel the noxious stripping chemicals from her lungs. The ground was slippery with frost. Small patches of snow remained from the last storm. She leaned down to hold Paul's small mittened hand as they descended the brownstone steps to the sidewalk and made their way around the perimeter of the fenced park, with Helen and Goran trailing closely behind.

Luna glanced around, looking for someone she could subtly signal for help, but the square was deserted this wintry afternoon. Where were the walking tours and lumbering amphibious Duck boats when you needed them? She couldn't even spot any curtain twitchers at the windows of the two dozen Greek Revival houses lining the park. She longed to enter the central green space to give Paul a chance to run on its small patch of grass, but it was off-limits to everyone, including residents.

Peeking back at the far side of the square, she scanned the roofline of the houses next to Malik's. No visible roof decks. Only steep slate shingles, fifty feet above the hard brick sidewalk. Heights scared her. She already knew there was no access to the roof from her room, but she needed to go over every possibility. On to the next plan.

After Luna and Paul had made one complete circuit of the quadrangle, she turned to her guards. "We need more exercise. Can we head over to Acorn Street?"

If there were any tourists at all in Boston on a bitter February day, they'd be on the most photogenic street in the city, one block over, taking selfies.

"No, that's enough." Goran said. "You got your fresh air. Time to go back."

As Luna led her son to the townhouse, she saw in her peripheral vision a navy-blue SUV inching its way up Pinkney Street, one of the roads at either end of the square. The driver was a block away, too far for Luna to make eye contact.

The time is not right yet, her father's voice cautioned. *You need to appear docile, so Malik will continue to allow these small excursions.*

CHAPTER 21

GORKA'S BAR

Bushy Eyebrows and Mermaid Tattoo conferred on where to go, then led Iris and Ash two blocks down Huntington Avenue to a shabby-looking bar called *Gorka's*.

"No one from the Academy will overhear us in this place," B.E. confided.

Iris could guess why the art students didn't frequent this place. The neon Pabst Blue Ribbon sign in the window and slightly sticky floor were ominous omens. It was approaching noon, but only a few patrons were scattered around the room, already drinking seriously. B.E. gestured toward a booth in the far corner.

Iris took a seat, then slid two sugar packets from a caddy under one of the table legs to stop its wobble. "I'm Iris, by the way. Can I buy you guys lunch?"

"Sure, thanks," M.T. said. "I'm Kiara."

"Zane," offered B.E.

A blackboard on the wall listed burgers, pizza, and tacos for menu choices, nothing vegan for Ash. A server approached, and they gave her their order. Iris and Ash stuck to coffee for her and tea for him.

Ash ran a hand through his hair. "So Cele had a baby? Who was the kid's father?"

Kiara looked down and scratched at the orange paint on her fingernail. "Whoever he was, he was out of the picture by the time Cele started in our program. Paul was maybe..." Kiara looked across at Zane, whose eyebrows were skeptically raised, "eighteen months old?"

Zane shrugged. "Sounds right. The little dude could walk and say a bunch of words. Cele paid some Northeastern student to watch him while we were in class."

Iris wondered how Luna had juggled motherhood with her required classes and studio work. "Did she have family supporting her? Does anyone know where she was from?"

Zane swept his eyes around the room, then leaned forward. "That's the funny thing. Cele was an incredible representational painter. Better than our instructors, even. She said she'd learned to paint in the old wet-on-wet style as a kid from watching her father work. He raised her somewhere on the South Shore and taught her to draw and paint. Cele told us he was dead now. He'd been her only family. Before Paul."

He removed his clear-framed glasses, dipped a paper napkin in his water glass, and cleaned the lenses. Then he held them up to the light and put them back on. "But if her father was that good of an artist, wouldn't we have heard about him? I asked her once what his name was, but she just changed the subject."

Kiara stared at Ash. "You say Cele was hiding things when she lived with you, but she was already a mystery woman here at art school. And we were her closest friends."

The server brought their food and drinks. Iris tore open a cream packet and poured a splash into her coffee. She was hungry and wished she'd ordered a hamburger like Kiara and Zane. "You must remember something that can help us find her. Some detail she may have let drop. Did she go out with anyone last year? Or was there someone who followed her around, maybe trying to get her attention?"

Kiara swallowed a bite of her hamburger and chewed. "I never saw her hanging with anyone. And we were living in the moment, not asking each other about our pasts. That wouldn't have been cool." She reached for a french fry and held it up in the air. "It *was* weird that Cele never put anything on social. The rest of us were all on TikTok and Insta, showing off our work, hustling to try to get discovered by a gallery. But for Cele, it was like she wanted to hide her talent."

The smell of the hot, greasy potatoes and grilled meat was making Iris salivate. She tried not to reach across the table and grab one of Kiara's french fries. "Did any of the instructors pay particular attention to her?"

Zane cocked his head. "All of us in the painting block had to take a course on nineteenth-century oil painting techniques. This was right up Cele's alley. The instructor was super impressed with her work. The school even bought her final painting for its permanent collection. Remember, Ki?"

"Yeah, Audrey Glenn thought Cele walked on water."

"That's the instructor's name, Audrey Glenn?" Iris thumbed it into the notes section of her phone, as she simultaneously exchanged cell phone numbers with Kiara and Zane.

"Right," Zane said. "Glenn with two 'n's.'" By then, his plate was empty. He checked the time on his phone. "We have to get back by one for our Chemical Composition class."

"Just a few more questions, okay?" Ash said. "Did Paul's father ever show up to visit the kid? He could have used Paul to lure Cele out of my building last Friday. Do you think he lived in the same town on the South Shore where Cele grew up?"

"Sorry, man. That's all I can remember. But thanks for lunch." Zane drained his bottle of Sam Adams and rose to his feet.

Kiara stood up too and gave them a quick wave. "Tell us when you find Cele. Now I'm really worried."

After they left, Iris asked Ash, "Do you have time if I order us some fries? We can go over what we just learned. Unless you need to get back?"

"No, that's cool. I'm in no rush. Hopefully, Kevin's not using any of my paintings as scratching posts."

The server walked over with the check but stuck it back in her apron pocket as Iris added a large serving of french fries and more tea for Ash to the tab.

Iris studied the notes on her phone. "One big revelation is that Luna went by the name Celia Núñez last year when she was in art school. That may or may not be her real name. But let's keep calling her Luna since that's how you think of her."

Ash nodded. "Second, we now know that Luna is Paul's mother. Father's identity is unknown."

Iris sat up straight when the french fries arrived. She squirted ketchup along one side of the plate. "These are for you, too. They're vegan, right?"

"Possibly."

After Iris and Ash had demolished half the order, she continued. "Maybe Detective Stroud can use police databases to track down a baby named Paul, born to a single mother somewhere on the South Shore three years ago. Or she could have been married to the guy. It would help if we knew Paul's birthday, and if Paul was the child's name on his birth certificate. Zane or Kiara, I forget which, mentioned a Northeastern student who babysat him. I wonder if they remember her name. The sitter might have more information."

Iris went to her phone's contact list. "I'll text them the question, since they're probably back in class now."

"What else?" Ash said. "Oh, the father who raised Luna. A talented painter living on the South Shore. Maybe he exhibited his work at a gallery. Do you think Stroud could dig out information about him—or an obituary?"

"Hey, the father could have left his house to Luna. Maybe she's there now."

Ash frowned. "No, when she called me, she asked for my help. She sounded terrified. I know someone's taken her, but I don't know why or where."

Iris dragged another fry through the ketchup. "About that phone call, I've been wondering..."

"Why she called *me*?"

Iris picked her next words carefully. "Yeah. I know you were friends, *are* friends, but for her to call you first to rescue her, it just seems..."

"Like more than friends?" Ash wadded up his napkin and tossed it by his plate.

"And if you were, let's say, somewhat more than friends, wouldn't she have told you more about herself? Like about having a kid?"

Ash let out a very deep breath. "I should be straight with you."

CHAPTER 22

LUNA-SUNDAY

By Sunday morning, the base layer on the canvas was dry. Luna added another layer of primer before eating a simple breakfast of toast and a boiled egg. She was grateful for the large Styrofoam cup of black coffee. Who was making her meals—the timid woman who delivered the tray? Could she arouse the woman's sympathy?

When the tray was removed, Luna tried to catch the woman's eye, but she kept her gaze averted and shut the door quickly. Malik must have warned her not to communicate with the prisoner.

Luna gently touched the surface of the canvas with her finger to ensure that the primer had set. The original Sargent sat on its easel next to the primed canvas. Holding a stick of soft charcoal, she hesitated, intimidated by the task ahead. She closed her eyes and tried to imagine how her father would advise her to begin this daunting task.

Divide it into quadrants, the way I taught you. Focus on one small area at a time.

Luna took a deep breath and proceeded to sketch the boy's outline in swift strokes, wiping the lines with a dry rag until they were barely visible, working steadily. After she was satisfied with the massing and placement of the figure, she added the toy boat.

Standing back from the easels, she compared the two paintings. Deciding that her sketch's spacing and volumes were accurate, she took a break. She sat on the floor with her back up against a wall, trying to work out the muscle kinks from the previous day.

Her mind drifted back to her childhood in Rhode Island, long before she got pregnant, before her father and boyfriend were murdered. It was a different lifetime. She used to worry about silly things, like what to wear to school, what the other girls were saying about her, whether she would pass her math test. She wanted to go back to being that girl. To have every possibility ahead of her, not so far out of reach.

Would she and Joey have stayed together? Probably not. Even then, she sensed that her sweet, handsome boyfriend was not the sharpest knife in the drawer. Unlike Ash, who was the full package. She allowed herself a moment or two to daydream about a life with him.

Then, Luna forced herself back to examining where she had taken the wrong path. A path that led her and Paul to this town-house prison, with her performing slave labor while communing with her dead father. She never should have agreed to copy that first painting for Malik.

After breaking for lunch, delivered and removed as breakfast had been, Luna rose stiffly from the floor to resume work. She started underpainting the context tone, laying a monotone wash on top of the sketched outlines. The raw umber and turpentine in the mixture would allow it to dry relatively quickly.

By late afternoon, she'd finished adding mid-range tones for the background just as Malik showed up to check her progress. He examined her work without speaking, his eyes travelling back and forth between her canvas and the original. Goran stood in the open doorway, talking quietly on his phone.

Watching him, Luna had a thought. Was there any way she could get her hands on a phone, Goran's or Helen's, to call for help?

But then she realized: who would she call?

CHAPTER 23

MORE THAN FRIENDS

Iris stared across the table at Ash. Noting the strain in his distinctive blue eyes, Luc's eyes, made her want to fix whatever was wrong.

"You don't have to tell me if you don't want to," she said. "I get that Luna is important to you, and you need to find her. That's all I need to know."

Ash started shredding a paper napkin into tiny pieces, not meeting her eyes. "No, I owe you an explanation. You're helping me try to find a woman, and you probably don't understand why I'm going to such effort." He cleared his throat. "This last year has been incredible: being with Raven, having you transform my run-down building and, OMG, learning that Luc is the father that my mother was keeping from me. Then, graduating college and getting my first gallery show. It's all been wicked intense, like a decade shrunk into a year."

Iris nodded, wondering where he was going with this, hoping it wasn't where she suspected.

"I've had to grow up fast, deal with all these huge changes. At the same time, I'm trying to find my artistic vision." He finally looked up at Iris. "Lately, it feels like Raven and I are in different places with our lives, you know?" He quickly added, "Through no fault of hers."

Iris' stomach clenched. "Her priorities may change after she graduates. College can be all-consuming. Have you talked to her about this?"

"I've tried. She just changes the subject. Raven thinks she's going to move in with me in May after she finishes RISD and moves home from Providence."

"But now Luna is in the picture?"

Ash's gaze turned back to his pile of napkin remnants. "It's not just that. Raven and I were drifting apart before Luna arrived. And I didn't mean for anything to happen. I'm not a player, I swear. But Luna and I started talking about our art and asking each other's opinions about stuff. We gradually realized how much we had in common." He blushed. "Yeah, and one thing led to another."

Shit, Iris thought. This is the first serious relationship Raven's had. If Ash splits up with her, it will break her heart. Damn this Luna Esposito, or whatever her real name is.

They sat in silence for a few moments before Ash continued, "I know there was a lot of stuff Luna didn't share with me. Things with us were just getting started. And now I may never see her again."

Iris wondered, what *were* their chances of finding this mysterious woman? "Ash, I'll help you look for Luna, but whether or not we find her, promise me you'll level with Raven about your feelings. Who knows? Maybe you two can work things out." *Iris Reid — architect and relationship counselor.*

"I will. It's just I don't want to hurt her."

Iris forced a smile. *Maybe a bit late for that.*

CHAPTER 24
LUNA-MONDAY

The real painting began on Monday morning. After breakfast, Luna mixed alizarin crimson, flake white, yellow ochre and some ivory black on her palette to create a middle value for the boy's skin. She held it up to the original painting and squinted.

Does this match, Papa?

A bit more crimson. Sargent gave this boy a rosy complexion.

Luna adjusted the shade until it matched the boy's underlying tone. She used a medium filbert brush to apply color in thin layers for the face. Then she moved on to the hands and legs. When she was satisfied with those foundation colors, she remixed more paint to mass in the hair and sailor suit, blocking in the simplified forms.

That afternoon, Malik nodded approvingly at her progress. As Goran led her down from the attic room to the third floor, Luna focused on putting her plan into action. Since Goran kept his phone in his back pants pocket under the tail of his jacket, she doubted she'd ever be able to slide it out without him noticing. Plus, he carried a gun. Instead, she set sights on grabbing Helen's phone while it was still unlocked. This would be tricky. Three things would need to line up perfectly. If they happened today, she had to be ready.

Goran knocked two times, his usual signal, and Helen unlocked the door. Paul stood across the room, staring out one of its windows at the light snow falling. She ran over to hug him, and he reached for her. "Why are we here, Mama? I want to go home."

"We will soon," she whispered into his hair as she held him close.

Goran stomped back out into the hallway, closing the door behind him, and Helen returned to the single comfortable chair to resume reading her romance novel. The woman seemed to have an endless supply of these paperbacks, each with a different bare-chested man on the cover. She wondered how much Helen inter-acted with Paul during their long days together.

Luna had studied the room's layout. It was high-ceilinged, although not as high as on the lower floors. The bathroom was en-suite, and Helen had set up a hot plate on a nearby table for her tea kettle, not a great idea for safety around a young child. Twin beds were lined up head-to-toe against the interior wall. Luna hated the thought of this cold, uncaring woman sleeping so close to her boy.

Malik had supplied some toys and books for Paul: blocks and trucks—typical boy things. But with no one for him to play with and no one to read to him, Paul had already grown bored. On her supplies list, Luna had requested a stuffed pig for Paul to replace the one he'd had to leave behind at Basia's. At least he had that. The boy clutched the new pig under one arm while anxiously sucking his thumb, a habit he'd long grown out of.

Luna sat cross-legged on the floor. "Come here, love. Sit on Mama's lap and I'll tell you a story."

Paul removed his thumb as he seated himself. "The one with the tree house?"

"No. You know you get a new story each day. That way, you'll have lots and lots of stories in your head to think about when I'm not here."

Over the last two days, things had settled into a rhythm of sorts. In the afternoons, after Malik approved her afternoon visit with Paul, she would spend half an hour in the boy's room telling him a story and playing with him while Helen read her bodice-rippers and talked on her phone. Then mother and son would bundle up to walk around Louisburg Square, accompanied by their two guards. Luna saw only one possible opportunity in that routine to gain access to Helen's unlocked phone.

Helen sipped a cup of tea, ensconced in her book. The phone sat on the table by the hot plate. Luna began her story about a pirate ship full of little boys, with a certain brown-haired one in charge. Paul wouldn't know she was riffing off Peter Pan. His thumb was back in his mouth as he listened intently.

Helen turned a page without shifting her gaze.

Luna's imagined boy-pirate was teaching the other kids how to fly. Did Luna remember J.M. Barrie's plot? Didn't matter. "A little green-winged fairy led the pirate crew off the boat. They flew over to an island."

Helen took another sip of tea.

"The pirates landed on the island and discovered a feast laid out on long tables in the sand. There were cupcakes, and peanut butter sandwiches, chicken nuggets, and cheeseburgers..."

"And ice cream?"

"Ten different flavors of ice cream."

Helen started to stand up. Luna kept her eyes on Paul.

"But then the green fairy told the boys that they should fill their pockets with the treats and sneak off into the palm trees to hide."

Helen checked something on her phone, laid it on the table, then retreated to the bathroom, closing the door.

Luna put a finger to her lips to keep Paul quiet, leapt up and tiptoed over to Helen's phone just before it powered off. She went to the keypad, quickly punched in Ash's number, and prayed that he would answer.

He did.

"Ash." The word came out in a whisper. "It's Luna. I need your help."

"Where are you?"

"I'm —"

The door creaked open. Helen's eyes widened. Enraged, she flew at Luna. Helen grabbed the phone and backhanded Luna sharply across the cheek.

Paul burst into tears.

CHAPTER 25

LUNA-MONDAY

Luna felt so defeated she couldn't even cry. Goran had tossed her roughly back into her garret. She'd landed hard on the floor, bruising her right thigh, and she remained lying there in a fetal position, staring up at the skylights. The thought of Paul witnessing his mother being struck by the woman in charge of him, then grabbed by Goran, made Luna shiver. This imprisonment must be traumatizing her young son. When would she see him again? Or would Malik now keep them separated until the forgery was finished to his satisfaction?

She couldn't help going over it: how Malik had managed to ensnare her six months ago. It had started out innocently enough. He was a friend of her instructor, Audrey Glenn, and had visited her art class to critique the student paintings. Later, over the summer break, he'd called her out of the blue with a business proposition. Luna had initially been flattered.

Malik Saban was a hotshot art appraiser used by all the big auction houses, museums, and wealthy art collectors to validate and appraise paintings from the late nineteenth and early-twentieth century. That was his specialty. The students knew his reputation. He summoned her to his opulent Beacon Hill townhouse to discuss having her copy some paintings for him. He'd assured her that these were for his own enjoyment and would never be represented as originals. She'd had some doubts, but her bank account was dangerously low, tuition for a second year at the art academy was due, and she had a young child to care for.

Malik had been a gentleman at first. Luna had even found him somewhat attractive for an older guy. But after she'd agreed to the job, when he gave her the James Whistler self-portrait to copy, along with a third-rate vintage painting to strip and use its canvas as a base, the genteel fiction was over. They exchanged looks, but she raised no objections. Especially after he asked about her son. She'd never mentioned Paul to him. Did Malik know who her father was, or was he just taking advantage of a talented student who needed money? He emphasized that discretion was essential since the collectors who submitted artwork to him for appraisal would not approve of him copying them for his private gallery.

Malik had been pleased with her rendition of the Whistler. She had completed it in a month, working in her cramped apartment. It was a hot July, and she'd propped the small canvas on her fire escape in the sun to get the layers of varnish to harden quickly. She doubted that the final result could pass atomic absorption or mass spectrometry testing. But if the buyer of this forgery—and Luna wasn't kidding herself about what she was producing—wasn't too sophisticated, and if the renowned Malik Saban verified it met his standards, then her employer would probably pull off the con.

But could she be criminally implicated in his scheme? He'd told her that the copy was strictly for his private use. If all went south, could she claim naiveté? Not if the authorities learned who her father was.

Luna deposited the check for six thousand dollars into her bank account, and after it cleared, told Malik that she wouldn't be able to do any more work for him. It was August, and classes were starting soon. She would be too busy with schoolwork.

But Malik Saban had no intention of taking no for an answer. And that was when he kidnapped her and Paul the first time.

CHAPTER 26

MALIK-MONDAY

Malik sat by his living room fireplace and swirled the golden liquid in his cognac glass. He had a decision to make. One of timing, not of result. His young forger had a shelf life, but he had hoped to squeeze several more paintings out of her. Unfortunately, she'd now tried his patience one too many times. He would not let Celia jeopardize his long-term business operation.

Malik's present life had been constructed with precision and self-discipline. A school trip to a museum in nearby Izmir had ignited his interest in art, and changed the direction of his life. It hadn't been easy to extract himself from his small village in Turkey by way of a scholarship to the Royal College of Art in London. It had taken many calculated steps to impress teachers and polish his language skills to get there, but even so, the transition to the U.K. had been a huge culture shock. Luckily, he'd been able to charm his Art History tutor, Rupert, who had helped smooth out Malik's remaining rough edges.

Working in galleries on both sides of the Pond, he'd amassed contacts throughout the tight-knit art collecting world. He'd also been exposed to the seedier sides of art acquisition: secretive middlemen and unscrupulous collectors who didn't worry so much about legitimate provenance.

A decade ago, after he switched from selling art in retail galleries to appraising high-end pieces for institutions and individual collectors, Malik's lifestyle grew more luxurious. He set up a testing laboratory in the basement of his newly acquired Beacon Hill townhouse and insisted that pieces be left with him for evaluation. This arrangement would allow for an occasional switch of a forged painting for the original, depending on the sophistication of the owner. The only hiccup in his business plan was the critical need for a talented, and very discreet forger.

Eight years ago, Malik discovered one of these through his art world network. Oliver Sheridan lived by himself on the north shore of Massachusetts in a picturesque cottage. For a living, he painted portraits of Boston business magnates to hang in their corporate offices and welcomed the extra income from occasional off-the-books commissions. But two years ago, Oliver's work became sloppy. There was a Toulouse-Lautrec lithograph that was such an obvious copy that Malik couldn't swap it. Oliver had started drinking heavily. Malik couldn't risk his forger becoming loose lipped at a local bar, so he dispatched one of his subcontractors to pay the man a visit. A final visit.

But this personnel vacancy left Malik in a bad position. He had just purchased a summer house in Nantucket and didn't want to lose his new lifestyle. He'd heard rumors about a master forger who lived somewhere in New England, but his identity was a closely guarded secret. Malik made it known that he was willing to pay dearly for any information about this guy, but no one was talking. Then the gossip circulated that the man had been killed, when Malik was desperate to get his side business going again. He now had interested buyers, and he needed the cash flow.

When an acquaintance at the Boston Academy of Art invited Malik to critique the students' work in her technical painting class, he hadn't expected to discover a new talent. At best, he'd hoped for an introduction to some handsome art student for a future hookup. The class had been assigned to copy the technique of a well-known artist, and they all managed something credible. But he'd been staggered by the craftsmanship in one student's painting. Celia Núñez was clearly a prodigy. She'd managed to capture the luminosity and exact brushstrokes of Édouard Manet's *Olympia* with uncanny accuracy. Malik tried to play it cool, not dwelling too long on that particular canvas, but it was hard to focus on the other, lesser paintings around the room.

Who was this Celia Núñez, and where or how had she learned to paint like that? When pressed privately, the instructor told him that Celia's artist father had trained her from an early age. They'd lived somewhere on the South Shore of Massachusetts. The teacher mentioned that Celia was a single mother with a young child. Interesting. She could probably use some extra cash.

Malik put out feelers among his contacts to investigate the girl's background. If he were to offer her an opportunity to work for him, he wanted to know everything about her. Someone with this particular skill set seemed almost too perfect.

His team was unable to dig up much about Celia Núñez. She had a toddler son and lived in a cheap apartment near the art academy. There were no footprints at all for her father.

The following summer, when Malik approached her about copying a painting for him, Celia's expression told him she knew the score. But she accepted the commission anyway.

Malik had worried that Celia's lack of backstory, at least anything that he could discover, might mean she was a plant from a government agency like Interpol sent to entrap him. But surely, they would have come up with a better cover for her. And after Celia produced a most convincing rendition of the James McNeill Whistler self-portrait, he relaxed.

Maybe her mysterious background meant the opposite, that she had something of her own to hide. Good. That would mean she'd never go running to the police to turn him in because she wouldn't want them to look too closely at who she was.

The Whistler forgery had fetched a pretty penny from a Saudi prince with a large but very private collection. After Celia balked at doing any more copies for him, Malik regretted having to use force to keep her in his employ, but her skills were far too useful to let her slip away. While keeping control of her little boy necessitated hiring a nanny, it was worthwhile insurance to keep the artist tethered firmly to the townhouse. At least Malik had thought so.

In November, after Celia managed to escape with Paul and the nanny, he had immediately fled to Switzerland, frantically monitoring the situation at home to see if she would turn him in. When his contacts reported that no authorities appeared to be interested in him, Malik relaxed a bit. He must have been right. Celia wanted to stay out of their sights as much as he did.

Still, he wouldn't feel completely safe until he had Celia back under his authority. Three months later, after Goran was finally able to locate her and bring her back to the townhouse, Malik made sure to block any future paths for escape. The plan was to keep her there, turning out her fine forgeries for as long as possible, using access to her son as the incentive.

But the woman was too devious. Malik needed to find out who she had tried to call on Helen's phone. The Sargent would be the last damn thing she'd ever paint.

The boy, however, could stay. He'd raise Paul as his ward. He would grow to become a handsome young man, and Malik would be sure to educate the boy himself.

CHAPTER 27
UNACCEPTABLE BEHAVIOR

I ris pulled into the lot behind her Cambridge loft and parked. Ash thanked her for coming with him to the art academy, got out, and headed over to his car.

After he drove off and she climbed the stairs to her apartment, Iris could hear Luc's grunts and moans coming from the living room across the open floor plan. Sheba padded over to greet her and rolled over onto her back for a belly rub. After paying the dog some attention, Iris poured herself a glass of iced tea. She glanced over the kitchen island to see a grimacing Luc perform tricep stretches while a buff young man in skimpy gym shorts murmured encouragement.

Luc had broken his arm in Costa Rica while they were on vacation last month. Even though his cast had been removed, Luc still had to exercise his weakened muscles. The physical therapist gave Luc some final instructions for follow-up workouts, then packed up his equipment and left.

Iris offered Luc a glass of water. "Muscles still stiff?"

"Jack says I need to keep doing this PT for four to eight more weeks if I expect to regain full mobility in my arm. Damn! This is punishment for going on vacation. Never doing that again."

"We just need to skip *active* vacations. No heli-skiing, skydiving, zip lining, or bungee jumping."

"Doesn't leave much."

"Just eating and looking at architecture."

Luc laughed. "Same as when we're not on vacation. I should change out of these sweats and go downstairs to start the prep for dinner."

Iris reached out and gently touched his wrist. "Wait. If you have a minute, I'd like to catch you up on what Ash and I found out today."

Luc followed her to the sofa, and they settled in sideways, facing each other, legs touching. She related everything Zane and Kiara had told them about Luna, aka Celia.

"Luna has a kid Ash didn't know about? This woman gets more mysterious by the day."

"And there's another thing. After the art students left, Ash and I talked. He admitted that he and Luna had become, let's say, intimate. That's why she called him to ask for help."

"What?" Luc's mouth set into a hard line. "Did he break up with Raven?"

"No. But he promised he'd explain all this to her."

"I need to speak with that kid. This is unacceptable behavior. Doesn't he know that? Dammit, I should have been there to teach him how to treat women with respect."

Iris held up her palm, gesturing "stop". "He says he's already tried to talk with her, but she doesn't want to go there. Raven must sense that he's pulling away."

"Still, you don't get to move on until things are resolved. I'm going to call him."

"Please don't. Give him some time to discuss things with Raven. It's not like anything's actively going on with Luna right now."

"Yeah." Luc wrapped his fingers around the back of his neck. "Maybe it's just as well that she's out of the picture. A breakup is always worse when there's someone else visibly taking your place."

"Ash said he would deal with this. You need to trust him."

CHAPTER 28
MALIK-TUESDAY

Malik had slept little. Now he sat in the window seat of his sunny kitchen on the townhouse's ground level, sipping linden flower tea and nibbling toast with orange marmalade.

The previous night, Goran had connected the number Celia had called on Helen's phone to an Ashley Burke in Medford. The address was the same as where Goran had found Celia hiding. His henchman had emailed him a link to Burke's gallery write-up.

Ashley Burke was a twenty-one-year-old painter and, judging by a critique of a recent show of his work, genuinely talented. Malik studied some photos of his paintings on the gallery site. They were quite good, if a bit wildly expressionistic for his taste. There was a photo of the artist as well. Gorgeous guy—looked to be mixed race with dreads and striking blue eyes, ripped physique. No wonder Luna went running to him.

How much had she told the handsome Ashley about who she was hiding from and why?

Would he really have to take care of Burke as well? What a waste.

CHAPTER 29

MALIK-TUESDAY

When Ash slotted his station wagon into a space in the lot behind his building, he automatically looked over to see if the lights were on in Luna's studio. Of course, they weren't. His heart ached. Would he ever see her again?

He entered the hall and hesitated outside her door. Sighing, he inserted his master key into the lock. Luna's studio smelled like oil paint, yet there was still a hint of her sexy perfume. He switched on the lights to be greeted by the eight large paintings propped up along the room's outside walls like a surrounding army. The ghostly eyes of the figures trapped under washes of paint drilled into him, accusing him of not looking hard enough for Luna. The young woman in the unfinished painting on the easel in front of him, Vermeer's *Girl with a Pearl Earring*, shot Ash a dismissive look over her shoulder, as if asking *How can you love her if you don't really know her?*

Ash lowered himself onto the daybed where, six days ago, he'd woken lying next to Luna. He'd studied her face as she slept, trying to memorize it so he could paint her later. When she'd opened her eyes to see him there, her legs still intertwined with his, she'd stiffened, a look of sheer panic crossing her features.

"What's wrong?" He'd asked, rising to his elbows.

A nervous smile appeared. "Nothing. I'm just not used to... waking up with anyone."

"Should I leave?"

"No, stay. I'll make us coffee." She'd risen. Ash watched her nude form disappear into the bathroom. He resolved to paint her from that angle as well.

Now, replaying that last time with Luna, he closed his eyes and brought her pillow to his nose, inhaling her scent. Exotic and mysterious, like her. So many secrets. *Why didn't you tell me about your son? I wouldn't have been scared off. And why didn't the boy live with you?*

An assertive knocking on the door jolted him from the bed. At first, he imagined he had willed Luna into returning. But when he answered the knocking, it was Reilly who stood in the hall, wearing her usual stained overalls, a do-rag on her head.

"Oh, it's you," she said. "I heard the door bang and wondered..."

"No, Luna's not back. I was just hoping to find some clues about where she'd gone. You haven't heard anything, have you?"

"Nope." Reilly brushed past him into the studio and glanced around at the paintings. "Holy shit." She approached the closest canvas and squinted. "And I thought my constructions were creepy. It's like people are trapped inside the paintings."

"That's why the series is called *Prisoners.*"

"Got it. Figural art overshadowed by abstract art. Very symbolic."

Reilly looked over Ash's shoulder and ran to the window. She waved her arms. "Hey, Muthaf—er. Whatcha looking at, voyeur!"

Ash scurried after her. "Who? Where?"

"That bald guy. Now he's running away."

"Pervert!" she screamed at the window."

"Chill, Reilly! He can't hear you."

"Dude was wearing some weird spy glasses." Reilly raised an eyebrow suggestively at Ash. "Maybe we should have put on a show for him." She sashayed back to Luna's unfinished Vermeer painting and tipped her head while she studied it. "You gotta admit, Luna's got some real painting chops. She could make serious money as an art forger."

CHAPTER 30
GORAN-WEDNESDAY

G oran cruised around the block, looking for a parking space, when he spotted Ashley Burke entering his building. He recognized the artist from his online social media presence. Goran couldn't risk anyone spotting the Audi in the studio's parking lot, not after the last time he'd been here, when Celia had made all that racket. For all he knew, the cops were already searching for her.

He parked two blocks away in front of a crunchy café called The Healthy Planet or something and was tempted to get a sandwich to-go, but they probably just served sprouts and tofu. He'd kill for a cup of Dunkin' regular and a jelly donut.

It was now dusk, and the streetlights were turning on. Goran walked two blocks to Burke's property, his pale gray eyes scanning the area for anyone keeping Celia's apartment under surveillance. But he saw only a couple of people bundled up in parkas, rushing along the sidewalks, staring down at their phones.

He was the one who'd uncovered the link between Celia and Burke. On Malik's little team, he was the one with the computer skills, although performing a reverse-search of the call on the nanny's phone was ridiculously easy. But Malik, being ancient, or at least in his early fiftties, seemed unable to manage even a simple browser search. Fine with Goran. He needed to remain indispensable to his boss. Mysterious subcontractors chauffeured away employees who'd lost their usefulness to Malik, never to be seen again. Like the boss' first forger, that old drunk. And now, he suspected Celia would suffer the same fate. Tough on the little kid, though.

Goran kept to the sidewalk as he approached the brick warehouse, looking for some sign of Burke. Before Goran could report to Malik, he had to ensure that his quarry hadn't slipped away.

The large industrial windows put the interiors of the units on full view. One studio was lit up on this side. Goran retrieved the special glasses from his coat pocket. They were less conspicuous than binoculars. He adjusted the setting on the glasses to zoom in. God, this apartment looked like a junkyard. Building supplies and construction equipment littered the space. Other than a bed and a tiny kitchen, the rest of the unit was devoted to creating hideous collections of random materials. Was this supposed to be art? While all the apartment's lights were blazing, no one appeared to be inside.

The adjacent unit was almost dark, with just a dim light in the kitchenette. Goran almost jumped in alarm as two glowing eyes glared back at him from the kitchen counter. A huge cat.

He shuddered, but kept walking, rounding the property to see another unit brightly lit. From his previous reconnaissance, he knew that this was Celia's place. Burke was standing in the middle of the room, next to an Asian woman with short red hair. They were staring intently at one of Celia's paintings.

Oh, damn. The woman spotted him. Time to disappear.

CHAPTER 31
A FRISSON OF FEAR

The next day, Iris headed to her office early. Her meeting with the new clients, the Petersons, wasn't until noon, but first, she wanted to jot down everything she knew about Luna Esposito, or whatever her name was. There had to be a way of finding this woman. Wasn't it almost impossible these days to stay completely off the grid?

Iris closed her office door as a signal to Rollo and Loretta, though yet to arrive, that she didn't want to be interrupted. Sheba lumbered over to her dog bed in the corner and lay down, head on her paws, watching her mistress intently.

Iris retrieved a yellow pad and razor point pen out of her desk drawer, preferring to write her list out on paper, old-school. She couldn't rid herself of the fear that she was missing something important, maybe something dangerous.

A while later, she had listed things to investigate further. Loretta tapped lightly on the glass office door and held up a coffee mug, oblivious to the meaning of a firmly closed door. Iris shook her head, not wanting to break her concentration.

Had Ash told Detective Stroud about their discoveries the previous day at the art academy? Iris chewed on the end of her pen. Did the detective have any information for them?

Damn! What was she missing? She gazed out through her interior window and watched Rollo talking on his phone. The phone call from Luna! If someone had interrupted the call by snatching the phone away, the snatcher could find out who Luna had called for help. Maybe do that *69 trick. Could they track down Ash through his phone number? If they didn't know how much Luna might have revealed, Ash would be viewed as a threat.

A frisson of fear prickled across her back. Whoever took Luna might come after Ash next.

CHAPTER 32

A NEW LEAD

Iris tried calling Ash, but it went straight to voicemail. She texted him:

Call me.

The Petersons were due to arrive at any minute. In fact, through her office's glass door, she saw a middle-aged couple by the reception desk handing their coats to her office manager.

Loretta led the two toward the conference room, where they stopped outside the door to admire the model of Alex Harcon's museum displayed on its pedestal. Iris stood up, smoothed the skirt of her suit, tossed Sheba a bone to keep her occupied, and walked out to join them. They exchanged introductions, and Iris gestured for them to take their choice of seats around the conference table. Rollo hesitated a moment at the door, then entered, carrying his laptop to take notes. He shook hands with the Petersons. Loretta followed him in and offered everyone the coffee and refreshments she'd laid out earlier on the credenza.

Iris had a good feeling about these new clients. Anna Peterson, sporting giant, red-framed glasses, reminded her of her friend Ellie, who was funny and smart. Jack Peterson seemed more understated, dressed down in a sports coat, jeans, and sneakers. Iris wondered if Anna was the driving force in decision-making in the couple, always important to figure out. The Petersons told her they had two grown kids who visited often, but without spouses or grandchildren yet.

Rollo displayed a slideshow of the firm's work on a screen on the far wall. Iris spent the next hour asking Anna and Jack to describe the kind of house they wanted. Modernist, featuring views of the ocean. The size should accommodate their visiting children and eventual grandchildren but still feel cozy when it was just the two of them. They expected the budget to be around two million. Iris asked some questions but preferred to listen to decipher the subtext of how they envisioned their dream house. She would later check in with Rollo to get his take on what he'd heard. Iris was still learning how much she could trust her employee's instincts on the crucial people-handling side of the job. She was used to relying on her own judgment and doing everything herself.

Ninety minutes later, as the meeting wound down, Rollo gave the Petersons a contract to review at home. Iris escorted them out with a promise to make a site visit to the property as soon as she received the go-ahead from the signed contract.

Iris and Rollo held a quick debrief at his desk in the open office while Loretta listened in. His interpretation of the clients' priorities was close to Iris' own. She asked Loretta to schedule their land surveyor to draw up a plot plan on the North Shore property as soon as the signed contract and retainer came in.

Returning to her office, Iris glanced at her phone and noticed that Ash hadn't responded yet to her text. She felt energized after her meeting, eager to unroll the familiar yellow tracing paper and start sketching floor plans right away. But she had learned the hard way to restrain herself until the clients were formally on board and she had a chance to see the site.

After setting up a preliminary file folder for the Petersons on the firm's network, and dragging in the notes from today's meeting, she returned to her concerns about Ash. The year before, he'd been in danger and had moved into Iris and Luc's loft for a few days. Back then, Ash had only recently learned that Luc was his father, and living together had felt awkward. Their relationship was more comfortable now, but Iris suspected Ash would still rather be in his own space, if it was safe.

Was their loft even a smart place for Ash to hide? If whoever had taken Luna had traced her phone call back to Ash, maybe that person had watched Iris and Ash visit the art academy the previous day and knew of Iris' connection to the search. Had she noticed anyone following them? Was she herself safe?

What should she do? She grabbed her cell phone and texted him again:

< Call me as soon as you get this. You might be in danger. >

Why hadn't Ash answered?

CHAPTER 33
AUDREY GLENN'S DENIAL

Just when Iris decided to drive to Medford to check on Ash, her phone buzzed. His name flashed on the screen. She breathed out in relief as she sat back down at her desk.

"Sorry, I had my phone on vibrate and missed your call," he said. "You said something about danger?"

"It occurred to me that whoever snatched the phone away from Luna could do a reverse-search to see who she'd dialed and find out where you live. He might think you'll try to rescue her."

"I would if Luna had told me where she was."

"But he may not know that she didn't blurt out the address as soon as you picked up."

"Whoever was close enough to grab the phone would have heard how little she was able to say."

Iris pinched the bridge of her nose. "But because of that phone call, you're on their radar as a possible threat. Maybe you should come stay with us for a while. Just to play it safe. My home office is empty. You could bring your stuff and paint in there."

It was a moment before Ash responded. "Thanks. That's a nice offer, but I think I'm okay here. There was a guy Reilly thought she saw... never mind. She's a little paranoid. I'll let you know if I dig up any more information or if Detective Stroud calls, and you do the same, okay? I'll be fine."

"At least stay inside your loft and don't answer the door. You can have food delivered and left outside your entry."

"Don't worry. I'll be fine."

Iris set down her phone and reached into her desk drawer for the bottle of aspirin. *Why do young people always think they're immortal?* She dry-swallowed two tablets. Maybe she was being alarmist. She stared down at the list she'd made that morning on her yellow pad. At least she could be productive by checking on a few of the items:

1. The artist father - surname Núñez?
2. Galleries on South Shore - talented figurative painter who had recently passed away?
3. Audrey Glenn - instructor for the painting techniques class. Had she kept in touch with Luna, or did she know any more details about her past?
4. The babysitter, a Northeastern student - how to find? Did Northeastern have an online jobs board she could search? Zane and Kiara had texted back that they couldn't remember her name.
5. Basia Sobieski - Had Detective Stroud turned up any background information by now? Where and how had Luna met her? Had there been any identifiable fingerprints in her apartment left by her killer?

Iris decided to tackle #3 first. She found the art academy's website and a photo of a frizzy-haired woman beside a phone number for

Audrey Glenn. The woman looked familiar. Wait—wasn't she the first person at the art academy to whom they'd shown the photo of Luna? She'd said she didn't recognize her. Had they asked her about Luna Esposito or Celia Núñez? Or maybe they hadn't said a name, just showed her photo. Kiara and Zane did say that the Luna in the photo had changed a lot since they'd last seen her at school.

She punched in Audrey Glenn's number and was relieved when a woman's voice answered.

Iris explained that she was a friend of Celia Núñez and was trying to locate her. She'd heard that Ms. Glenn was a favorite instructor of Celia's and might know her present whereabouts. She hoped that a little flattery might distract the instructor from her flimsy rationale for looking for Luna.

"Did you tell me your name?" Ms. Glenn asked.

"My name is Iris Reid. Celia was supposed to meet up with me last week, but she never showed and hasn't returned to her apartment. Her friends and I are worried about her. But when we tried to think about where she'd go, we realized we didn't know that much about her background. Someone mentioned that she'd often talked with you last year at school, and we were hoping you might have some idea. Or maybe she's contacted you?"

"How strange. I hope she's okay. I haven't seen or heard from her since she took my class last year. Is her son missing as well?"

"Yes, Paul is gone too, but she left her cat behind." *Was she telling this stranger too much?*

"That doesn't sound good. Have you reported this to the police?"

"They think she's just gone off on a vacation and forgot about the cat. But as a pet owner, I can't imagine that."

"No, me neither. I wish I could help, but Celia told me nothing about her past."

"What about her father? I know he was an artist who'd taught her to paint. Do you know his name or where he lived?"

"Celia said he'd passed on but never mentioned his name. I'm sorry, I have a class to teach now, so I must run. Good luck finding her."

Iris crossed out Audrey Glenn's name. She had been no help.

CHAPTER 34

MALIK-THURSDAY

Malik's eyebrows rose as he saw the name on the Caller ID of his phone, buzzing itself off the arm of his chair. That woman was such a nuisance, always thinking of flimsy excuses to call him. Maybe he should just tell her he was gay and get rid of her once and for all. He motioned for his hairstylist to pause his clacking scissors while Malik took the call. The stylist silently retreated from the kitchen back into the town-house's central hall, closing the door quietly behind him.

"Audrey, what a surprise to hear from you. How's your winter semester coming along? I hope you have one or two students worthy of your expertise."

He listened for a minute. "Yes, I think I remember her." He straightened in his chair, frowning.

The woman went on.

"How strange. Were you close to Celia Núñez? Why would this friend of hers call you?"

"Uh-huh... uh-huh. What was the friend's name? Irene Reed, you think? No, I never encountered that Celia student after the critique last year. I remember being impressed by her work, though. I hope she turns up. Of course, I'll let you know if I hear anything through my art-world network. Take care."

After Malik got his breathing back under control, he called Julian to come back in to finish his haircut.

The unfortunate fallout from using Celia Núñez as his forger was growing. First, he'd had to have the cleaners get rid of the duplicitous nanny, Basia Sobieski. And now, after finishing the Sargent canvas, Celia herself would have to go. Was he going to have to eliminate Ashley Burke and this Irene Reed woman who were searching for Celia as well? Surely so many disappearances would attract attention.

Helen had assured Malik that Celia hadn't had time to say anything relevant to Burke, but Malik had Goran follow the guy anyway to make sure he couldn't discover where she had called from. And it turned out Burke went to the art academy, probably trying to pick up Celia's trail. He was there with some woman. Was it the same woman who'd contacted Audrey? They were getting too close for comfort. Malik tried to suppress his mounting sense of unease.

With enough determination, those two might actually stumble onto Celia's whereabouts. Hopefully, Celia's body would be gone before that could happen.

CHAPTER 35

LUNA-THURSDAY

Luna dabbed the skinny brush in the white flake paint on her palette and added a tiny dot to the middle of the boy's pupils to mimic the reflection of light. She stood back and stared critically at the canvas. She'd finished the background yesterday and started on the face this morning. Now, she was trying to capture the rest of the boy's features.

But the eyes were wrong. She kept painting Paul's haunted ones instead of copying the original painting in front of her. She couldn't stop worrying about what had happened to her son since she'd last seen him three days ago. This was torture. She didn't hear any crying coming from the room below. No noise at all. Had Malik sent Paul away?

Since the incident on Monday, Malik had Goran accompany him in Luna's studio on his afternoon progress visits. That decision shot down her idea of stabbing him with the sharpened end of her biggest paintbrush. She'd visualized so clearly spearing him in the throat and watching blood spurt out. But she could never take on two men, especially when one of them packed a gun.

Luna was now so tired her vision was blurring. She'd barely slept the last three nights and felt like curling up on the floor, giving up. How could she plan her next move if her mind kept swimming like this? She needed Papa's guidance.

You must keep it together, child! Your chance to escape will come soon, and you need to be ready.

But I'm so tired, Papa. And they've taken Paul. I can't run away without him.

She still had most of the money her father had left her, hidden in a safe deposit box. If she and Paul could escape a second time, they would use that money to go far away, maybe to Canada.

Soon she would be allowed downstairs to bake her forgery in the converted pizza oven. The process would take a series of three-hour sessions over five or six days. Surely Goran's attention would wander during some of that time. But this plan would work only if she could figure out how to free Paul.

Footsteps sounded on the stairs, and her insides lurched. The latch clicked, and the door swung open. Malik stood there, glancing briefly at her before moving over to the easel. Goran entered behind him and closed the door. Luna stepped back nervously, offering a blank expression. Malik's hard gaze traveled back and forth between the Sargent and her copy before he frowned. "The eyes are wrong. Fix them."

"Where is my son? I want to see him now."

Malik lifted his brows. "You're hardly in a position to issue demands."

"Do you want your fake Sargent finished or not?" Luna blinked. She hadn't planned on giving him an ultimatum.

He gave her a tight smile. "I have Paul safely tucked away. And

I'm sure I can find another artist willing to finish this job." With that, he turned and left the room. Luna heard the dull thud of the door closing and the lock click shut.

Had she pushed him too far? What would happen to her son if Malik really did get rid of her?

CHAPTER 36
PISCO MARTINIS

Iris had just finished compiling a list of a dozen or so likely art galleries on Massachusetts' South Shore when a text message popped up on her computer:

You have a guest at reception.

Through her office's interior window, she could see her friend Ellie. Iris immediately wondered if Ash had broken up with Raven and Ellie was here to discuss her daughter's shattered heart. But Ellie looked her usual upbeat self as Iris motioned her back to the office.

"So how did your meeting go with the new clients?" Ellie squatted down next to Iris' desk to scratch behind one of Sheba's floppy Basset ears. "Who's a good girl, huh?"

"I couldn't have conjured up a better project or a nicer set of clients if I'd tried. They even have a realistic budget for a completely new house on a tricky site overlooking the ocean."

Ellie squealed. "A miracle—we have to celebrate!" Her knees cracked as she straightened up. "Let's go down the street to the

Royal. You don't have any dinner plans, do you? I know Luc is busy at the restaurant on Thursday nights."

"Great idea. Let me ask Loretta if she can drop Sheba off at the loft on her way home."

With the dog's evening plans settled, she and Ellie advanced warily for a block and a half to the trendy Peruvian restaurant in Huron Village. The ground was slippery with frost. It was only five-thirty in the evening, and pitch dark, but a cosmopolitan after-work crowd was already filling up the high-ceilinged industrial space.

They hung their parkas on a coat rack and took seats at one of the zinc-covered tables by the front windows.

"I'm craving one of those Pisco martinis with horseradish," Ellie said.

"Sounds good." Iris studied the drinks menu. "I think I'll get a Royal Sour this time with Pisco and pomegranate."

Their server took the drink orders and bustled behind the busy open bar and kitchen.

"When do you and Mac leave for St. Lucia?" Iris asked, looking over the menu.

"Assuming he has no last-minute emergencies at the hospital, we take off in, uh, ten days. I can't wait to get away from this dreary snow."

"This winter hasn't seemed too bad." Iris cracked open a couple of pistachios and popped them into her mouth.

"That's because you just spent two weeks in Costa Rica."

When the server returned with their cocktails, they quickly ordered their meals.

Iris held up her remarkably pink drink. "Skål."

"Here's to Roku's next star of documentaries and the architect for another primo design commission!" Ellie said. They clinked glasses.

Iris took a sip. "I'd better go easy on these tonight. We're doing the final taping for the documentary tomorrow morning, and I don't want to look all puffy faced."

"Will Alex Harcon fly in for a guest appearance on this last segment? Doesn't he have to cut a big ribbon with giant scissors or something? And do you need Raven and me to impersonate your employees again?" Ellie held up a blue corn chip. "She's coming up from Providence to spend the weekend with Ash." Ellie couldn't conceal a smile of maternal pride.

Iris' breath caught in her throat. Should she tell her friend that Ash was intending to break up with Raven? She knew Ellie could never keep from alerting her daughter. "I think Harcon has figured out by now that you guys were just window dressing for the film and didn't really work for me. I can't wait for this documentary to be done," she said, trying to change the subject, but her feeling of guilt remained. Would Ellie feel betrayed when she learned Iris had been helping Ash search for a missing woman, his new love interest? And what about future occasions when Luc's son and Iris' goddaughter would inevitably run into each other at events? God, it would be so awkward.

"You okay? You look sick."

"I'm just panicking about the filming tomorrow. I hope I don't flub my lines in front of Alex. You need to help me decide what to wear. Ah, here's our food." Iris helped to clear space at the small table.

The server laid Ellie's lomo saltado neatly in front of her and placed the blue cod ceviche at Iris' place.

They spent the next few minutes eating in respectful silence before Iris held out her spoon toward Ellie. "Here, taste this. If you can parse the spices mixed up in here, you'll have Luc's eternal gratitude."

Ellie laughed. "The chef won't share his recipe with Luc?"

"It's a closely guarded secret." Iris glanced over at chef JuanMa, his back to the room as he pan-fried something on the open kitchen's blazing cooktop.

"They called this marinade tiger's milk on the menu." Ellie said. "Which is weird because there's no dairy in it. I'm no expert on South American spices, but I'll give it a try." She tipped the spoon into her mouth. "Well—definitely lime juice, fish stock, sweet peppers, and some hot ones, too. But wait, I know that taste." Ellie held up a finger. "Ginger!"

Iris smiled. "I think you're right. Mystery solved. My obsessive/compulsive chef thanks you."

"Maybe he'll make it for me next time we come for dinner."

After they finished every morsel on their plates, Ellie asked, "Should we have dessert? They have that caramel mousse with the fresh fruit that Raven likes so much."

"Sure, let's split one."

Ellie tipped her head, thinking out loud. "Raven's really looking forward to moving in with Ash after graduation this spring. He's such a nice guy, and I love him to pieces. But I've been thinking that his own studio will be tight quarters with them living there and both trying to paint during the day. Maybe one of the other tenants will move out. Wouldn't it be great if they had two of those studios so they could each have their own workspace?"

CHAPTER 37

A CHAT WITH THE DETECTIVE

Ash perched on a stool in his kitchenette, staring at his phone and debating. Kevin strutted across the floor nearby. It had been forty-eight hours since Ash had told Detective David Stroud about Luna's disappearance and its likely connection to Basia Sobieski's murder. He still hadn't heard anything back about developments in the case. It was high time to call Stroud to ask for a progress report. In exchange, he could tell the detective what he and Iris had learned the day before at the art academy.

He knew Stroud didn't want Ash interfering personally in the case, but if their information could help to find Luna, he'd risk being scolded. And maybe he should mention the man Reilly thought was watching them yesterday. Probably not. Stroud would think either Ash was being paranoid, or it would give him an excuse to isolate Ash from the investigation entirely.

Ash punched in the phone number and waited to be connected. When he reached the detective, he asked for news.

"I'm afraid I can't comment on an active investigation," Stroud said.

"Oh, come on. You wouldn't have even known that Sobieski had been murdered if it weren't for me. You thought it was just a burglary gone wrong." His voice started to crack. "You didn't hear Luna's voice on the phone. She sounded terrified."

"I know. And I do have a team working very hard on this."

"I've learned a few more things about Luna, including a different name she went by when she was at the art academy last year."

"You've been poking around on your own? I told you not to do that, Ash. These people have already shown that they're capable of violence."

"And they have Luna and her son! We don't have time to just plod along."

"The boy is Luna's son? You know that for sure?"

Ash sighed. "How 'bout this: I'm about to head out to the Healthy Planet for dinner. What if we bumped into each other there and just happened to chat over a meal? If it advances the search for Luna, what is the harm in that?"

After a few moments of silence, Stroud said, "I *am* getting hungry. Fine, I'll see you there in half an hour."

WHEN DETECTIVE STROUD ARRIVED, ASH WAS ALREADY SITTING IN A booth toward the back. Although the restaurant specialized in vegan, gluten-free, and otherwise healthy food, it resembled a neighborhood greasy spoon, its previous incarnation. Garlands of Christmas tree lights, its year-round décor, adorned the walls and cast a multi-colored hue.

"I've never been here before." Stroud shook Ash's hand and slid into the banquette across from him. The detective wore the same sports jacket as before and looked tired. "Is the food good?"

"*I* think so. I'm vegan."

Stroud picked up the menu. "You mean I can't get a burger?"

"A veggie burger."

Stroud frowned, still looking at the menu. "I'm not really here talking to you about the case, right?"

"No, man. We're shooting the breeze about the Celtics this season. How 'bout that Jayson Tatum?" Ash looked up as a young server approached and pulled out a small pad of paper from her apron pocket.

"Having your regular, Ash?"

"Yup." He looked over at his companion. "Do you know what you want?"

Stroud closed his menu and handed it to her. "The eggplant parm for me."

"You've got it."

After the server left, Stroud said, "You go first. You knew Luna had gone to the art academy last year?"

"After I spoke with you on Tuesday, I remembered her mentioning it. I thought I might find some of her friends there who might not want to talk to the police. There was a painting of hers in a group show that I recognized, but it had a different name listed for the artist: Celia Núñez. I showed the picture of Luna around and eventually found two students who knew her. They confirmed she was calling herself Celia Núñez then."

Stroud took a small notebook out of his jacket pocket and wrote down the name. "We can see what the school has on file for her contact information. You said the boy was around three years old? There must be birth records somewhere."

While they ate, between bites, Ash filled Stroud in on their other discoveries while the police officer jotted down notes.

After Ash had finished his buffalo tofu bowl, he said, "Okay, your turn. What have you found out?"

Stroud flipped to a different page in his notebook. "There were seven black Audi SQ8s sold in New England in the last few years, but none had tinted windows. We interviewed your tenant, and he was sure about the tinted part. The car might have been bought second-hand on the open market."

"Jess is a real car freak. His description would be accurate."

"We've been pursuing leads from the Basia Sobieski angle. Now that we've re-categorized her death as a murder/kidnapping case, we searched her apartment again and found a burner phone hidden inside a hair dye box. It showed calls made and received to another phone, probably another burner, possibly Luna's. Sobieski entered the country legally seven years ago and eventually got a driver's license with a Dorchester address. She paid taxes, listing her occupation as a nanny. We ran her through VICAP and NCIC to see if she had any criminal history, but she seems clean."

"Did you check out the Dorchester address?"

Stroud gave him a long-suffering look. "The apartment had changed tenants several times over the years. No one there knew anything about her."

"That's all you discovered? What about the boy?"

"Her Medford landlord said she claimed he was her grandson. We checked out the neighborhood, but apparently, they kept to themselves. After running Luna Esposito's name through our computer database, which covers the entire country, it got no hits. We don't know how her path intersected with Sobieski's. We don't even know if Luna was here legally. She could be undocumented. Too bad you didn't ask for more reference information when she came to rent from you."

"Yeah, I know." It wasn't a failure Ash felt like revisiting. He sipped his tea, considering the new information. "We didn't find a phone when we searched through Luna's apartment, but it might be hidden. What about calling the number on Sobieski's burner phone and seeing if it rings someplace in her studio, in the kitchen or wherever she might have hidden it? It might have calls on it from her kidnapper."

"Even if we could find Luna's burner, she probably just used it to call Sobieski."

"Still, it might be worth a try, right?"

CHAPTER 38

LUNA-FRIDAY

L una looked down at the plate of scrambled eggs on the tray the old woman had shoved inside the door. She had tried to catch the woman's eye, to plead somehow for her help, but she'd backed out of the room without looking up, quickly locking the door behind her. Malik was probably down in the dining room, sipping fresh-squeezed orange juice, nibbling on Eggs Benedict, maybe filling in a crossword puzzle while Luna suffered up here in her garret. Sitting cross-legged on the hard floor, she downed the cup of lukewarm black coffee, hoping to jump-start her brain cells.

How badly had she screwed up yesterday, demanding to see Paul? What had she been thinking? She had no leverage. Malik made that clear when he threatened to replace her. After their confrontation, Luna repainted the eyes in her forgery to match the Sargent boy's. Malik must know that the only steps remaining were the baking and glazing. Between now and then, she had to find a way to escape. And then she needed to find Paul.

She didn't notice the tear traveling down her cheek until the salty moisture mingled with her first bite of eggs. She'd considered going on a hunger strike, or stabbing the Sargent painting with the end of her paintbrush to tear the canvas, but with her son hidden away, what would that accomplish? The thought of Malik hurting Paul made her sick, but at least his threats had confirmed to her that Paul was still alive. Unless he was lying.

The lump in her throat made it hard to swallow the last of her breakfast. She almost choked. Why had she squandered her one chance to escape? She should have called the police when she got her hands on Helen's phone instead of wasting her call on Ash. Even if she couldn't blurt out her location, didn't the police have ways to track the source of a 9-1-1 call? Ash would never be able to find her.

She needed to come up with a plan. Had the big pizza oven arrived yet? Malik hadn't mentioned it or where it would be set up, but she would have heard crashing and bumping noises if something that unwieldy was carried up the stairs.

Luna thought back to the few times she'd been downstairs, in the townhouse. On the first level, she'd seen the grand living room and adjoining dining room. Was the kitchen in the back, or down in the basement like in a lot of Georgian houses? She vaguely remembered seeing a "garden level" under the front stoop on her walks outside. It was half a flight down from the sidewalk. That would be a logical spot for the oven to be set up. If it were there, maybe she could distract Goran long enough to climb out a window.

But how could she abandon Paul? Should she try to escape on her own from the basement or first floor, then get the police to return to capture Malik? If the police believed her, they might be able to compel him to say where he was keeping her son.

Luna finished her last bite of eggs and pitched the paper plate into the small trash basket. She was going to need all her strength for her escape attempt. She stood and took a few steps to her tiny half-bathroom to wash her hands. In that small space, she definitely smelled ripe. During the time she'd been in Malik's house, she'd only been able to give herself sponge baths. But now, she needed to pull herself together.

She returned to the room to begin her exercise routine, jogging laps around the small space and doing push-ups. After that, she would give herself a thorough washing.

Papa, I'm going to be brave. This may be my last chance to survive. If I see an opportunity to run, I need to take it. Then I'll find Paul.

CHAPTER 39
A PERFECT SETTING

At nine a.m. on Friday morning, Iris sat in the makeup chair in the atrium of the new Harvard Square Museum, reviewing her notes. As the stylist stroked on some eyebrow pencil, Iris watched Alex Harcon, in his bespoke suit, wandering around the grand space, grinning like a new father. The previous afternoon, pieces of his art collection had been moved from a Somerville warehouse and carefully mounted in their assigned exhibition spots. Alex placed a palm against the bronze surface of a ten-foot-high Douglas Abdell sculpture, placed in front of a wall of lush hanging greenery. "A perfect setting," he said.

Iris called over to him, "Alex, let's go over this script. You may want to make some tweaks."

The small film crew milled around, adjusting the lighting, performing sound checks, and confirming camera angles.

Alex was that rare billionaire who genuinely possessed an eye for fine art. He consulted with a highly qualified consultant, but he'd relied on his own judgment to amass the superb collection of modern American art which filled the museum. Iris hoped this Roku documentary about her creative process in designing it would be good publicity for the museum, for Milo, and for her.

Iris stood up, and the stylist quickly grabbed Milo by the arm as he was passing by. "Into the chair, pretty boy."

Milo was the only contractor Iris knew who moonlighted as the lead singer with a rock band by night and typically wore black leather pants to the construction site. His crew, who all looked like members of the Hells Angels, worshipped him. "I don't need make-up," he protested.

Ten minutes later, the make-up stylist had finished powdering the faces of both Milo and Alex Harcon, hair sprayed Milo's long black braid, and added some coverup under the eyes of the jet-lagged Harcon. An assistant clipped a microphone onto Iris' lapel.

She stepped gingerly between the tangle of video lights and wires, over to the foot of the curving sculptural staircase. The camera operator started with a wide pan across the atrium, then moved in for a close-up of Iris looking elegant in a white silk blouse and charcoal pants, hair loose around her shoulders. Leaning casually against the handrail, she went into a rehearsed recapping of her concepts for the design, the juxtaposition of different materials, and the orchestrated massing of architectural forms.

Alex Harcon then moved into the frame, feigning delight, acting as if he was seeing the finished building for the first time. Although based on his childlike expression half an hour before, it wasn't much of a sham. He described what he'd wanted to achieve in his museum and the types of artwork he'd showcased inside.

The third speaker was Milo, who led the cameraman and the sound guy on a tour through the building while discussing the construction process.

The three of them ended up together back in the atrium, each holding sparkling flutes of champagne that an unseen assistant had handed them. They turned to each other, toasted, and took a sip. Alex then encouraged everyone to come visit the new museum soon.

As soon as the showrunner called "Cut," Jason clapped enthusiastically. "Everything looked super, just super!"

Alex thanked him for documenting his labor of love. After the production crew packed up and disappeared into their vans, Alex invited Iris and Milo to lunch at the nearby Charles Hotel, where he had stayed the previous night.

Milo begged off. "I've got a rehearsal to go over a new song for our gig tonight. But it's been great working with you, Alex. You two go. I'll lock up here."

~

"MORE WINE?" ALEX HELD UP THE HALF-EMPTY BOTTLE OF Meursault.

"No thanks. I'm not much of a drinker at lunch," Iris demurred.

She took a bite of Dover sole and chewed thoughtfully. The project had turned out well, and her client was pleased. She hadn't made too much of a fool of herself in the documentary, despite its rocky beginning when a skeleton had been found under the floorboards. While they were filming! That notoriety might even have fanned interest in the program and the museum itself.

Harcon's collection looked great in the spaces she'd created. One room featured abstract paintings on three of the walls. It brought to mind Luna's impressive painting in the art academy's alumni show, and she thought again about Luna's father, who had passed along his talent and skills.

"Alex, I'm trying to find out about a painter, recently deceased, who worked in oils in a traditional style, like the old Masters and Impressionists. I know that's not what you collect, but would you have any idea how to find out where he might have shown his work? I think he lived on the South Shore of Massachusetts, somewhere between Boston and Rhode Island."

Alex dabbed the corners of his mouth with a napkin. "I can't imagine anyone painting nowadays in that style. You mean regurgitating those pseudo-Impressionist landscapes?" He shuddered. "There's a lot of that junk in galleries on the Cape, I suppose."

"I'm not sure what style he specialized in. I just know he taught his daughter how to replicate master artists like Manet and Vermeer perfectly."

"Maybe he was an art teacher. Or how about an art restorer for a museum? Although I can't imagine they could copy an entire painting."

"Actually, it's the daughter I'm trying to track down. I thought I might find out where she had grown up by learning about her father. The daughter can also reproduce Old Masters with uncanny accuracy."

Alex tilted his head in thought. "What an odd niche for two painters to pursue in this day and age. For one thing, it takes years to get really skillful. And the only way for all that effort to pay off would be to forge paintings and sell them on the black market. These days, fakes are a huge problem for collectors and museums. Unless I buy artwork directly from an artist, I always have the piece authenticated. God forbid anything in my new museum is fake." He shrugged. "But realistic copies are everywhere, even in the most reputable museums." Alex' eyes twinkled. "I've heard rumors that the Louvre's *Mona Lisa* is a fake!"

On that provocative note, Alex glanced at the time on his phone. "I need to get to my plane, but I'm glad we could celebrate the museum's completion. It's everything I was hoping for, Iris."

His words warmed Iris's heart.

They passed through the hotel's front doors into the weak February sunlight.

"Let's work together on another project soon," Alex called out as he headed over to his waiting driver, and Iris walked toward home.

CHAPTER 40

A PRICKLING IN HER LEGS

Despite the cold, Iris decided to jog up Mass Ave to her karate dojo instead of taking the Red Line subway. She zipped up her long parka and tugged her knit cap low on her forehead for the fifteen-minute fast-walk to Porter Square. The 2 p.m. sparring class would burn off some of the energy she was feeling after the satisfying conclusion of her latest project. If she returned to her office, it wasn't like she could begin working on the new design for the Petersons before receiving their signed contract and retainer, much as she might like to start generating ideas.

Iris spent the next hour perfecting her kata exercises and skirmishing with another brown belt. By the time she made a final bow to the sensei, she had worked up a pretty good sweat. She threw her parka over her white cotton gi, stepped out into the cold, and started walking the eight blocks back to the loft.

Halfway there, she felt the small hairs on the back of her neck rise. A prickling started in her legs, moved to the small of her back, and zoomed up her spine. Like being in the woods and hearing a twig snap behind you. Someone was watching her, setting off her body's alarm.

She ducked quickly into the *Paper Source* store and peeked out its front window from behind a massive display of Valentine's Day cards. Most pedestrians, wrapped inside their parkas against the icy wind, trudged along the sidewalk with their heads down. Except for one guy. A hatless bald man in a black raincoat had slowed down, his eyes darting from side to side. Iris backed further into the store, away from his line of vision. Why would anyone want to follow her?

"Do you have a back door?" Iris asked the startled salesperson at the cashier.

The young woman with the nose ring gestured behind her. "But it's not really public..."

The door didn't set off any alarms when Iris pushed through it and found herself out on a narrow side street. She balled up her red cap and scarf and hid them in front of her coat as she jogged up Arlington Street. She chanced a quick glance behind her but saw no one following.

Did this guy know where she lived and was he headed there? Iris took a circuitous route to the back of her property and hid behind a giant spruce tree, searching for any sign of someone lying in wait. Should she call the police? But what could she say? Had the guy really been following her, or was she being paranoid?

Just then, the restaurant's kitchen door opened, and jazz music spilled out. Luc appeared, lugging a large trash barrel. As he heaved its contents up into a dumpster, Iris rushed toward him.

He stepped back to regain his balance as she wrapped her arms around him. "Well, hi. What are you doing back here?"

"I'm just returning from the dojo. The filming this morning went really well. Gotta run."

Luc looked confused as she rushed past him through the

kitchen and out the door to their loft's private entry. She double-checked that their alarm system was on.

Sheba was waiting for her at the top of the stairs. Back in her own kitchen, Iris heated some milk on the stove to make a soothing cup of hot chocolate. Her heart was still racing. She spooned in the rich cocoa powder and swirled it with a whisk. Carrying the warm mug to the living room, she sank down onto the sofa, and Sheba jumped up to join her. The dog flopped over to offer her soft underbelly for petting. Iris obliged and gradually felt her heartbeat return to normal.

Should she have told Luc that a man might have been following her? She and Ash hadn't exactly been discrete when they'd flashed Luna's picture around the art academy. Had word gotten back to the kidnappers that she and Ash were trying to find Luna? Oh, God. This is just the kind of situation Luc had warned her not to get involved in.

Iris sipped her cocoa. If someone had been following her, were they following Ash as well? She'd tried to convince him last night to stay here for protection. But maybe their loft wasn't safe either if the kidnappers had identified both of them. What kind of dangerous world was Luna involved in?

Then she remembered Alex Harcon's suggestion at lunch that Luna's talent for reproducing old masters might indicate an involvement in creating forgeries. Could that be why Luna changed her name and why her background was turning out to be so murky?

Iris stared at her dog. "Am I going to have to tell Ash that he's gotten involved with a forger, Sheba?"

Why do I always have to be the bearer of bad news?

Sheba climbed up on Iris' thighs to nudge her head under Iris' hand. Iris absent-mindedly rubbed between the dog's ears.

Other than its modern setting, Luna's rendition of the Manet's

Olympia from the alumni show could certainly pass as a forgery. And her *Girl with the Pearl Earring* vignette was a dead ringer for Vermeer's original. Iris picked up her phone, scrolled to the photo she had taken of Luna's work in the art academy exhibit, and pinch-zoomed on it. Yup, it even had surface crackling like a painting from the actual nineteenth century. That was the sign of a meticulous and accurate copyist.

All the evidence suggested that Luna had been hiding from someone who had now caught up with her. Several days after she had gone missing, Luna had called Ash to beg for his help. So, whoever took her was keeping her alive. Why? For her exceptional painting skills?

Iris set her mug down on the coffee table. How could she find out about forgers and art traffickers in the New England area? She doubted Ash would know anything about the criminal side of the art world. She herself had had some dealings with an agent at the FBI the previous year, but suspected he'd never want to hear from her again.

Then she remembered Kelly Duval, a woman she'd met in Costa Rica last month at surf camp. Kelly worked for Interpol's Antiquities Trafficking Unit. She might be familiar with some of the players in this region.

Iris went to her home office and fished out a business card from her neatly organized drawer. Assuming Kelly was working at the family vineyard, her cover identity, it would be around one p.m. with the three-hour time difference between Massachusetts and California. Iris punched in the phone number.

"Duval Winery, Kelly speaking."

"Hi, it's Iris Reid. How is life at the vineyard?"

"Iris! It's good to hear from you. Life's actually pretty slow here in the winter. Are you and Luc planning a trip to come see us in Northern California?"

"No, unfortunately. I'm calling about something else. Luc's son, Ash, is an artist. He has a friend, Luna Esposito, who may have been kidnapped by some bad actors involved in art forgery. Luna is a very talented traditional painter and was taught to paint like the old masters by her father, who is now deceased."

"I thought you were an architect! Are you sure the building design gig isn't *your* cover?"

How do I keep getting pulled into these situations? "I made the mistake of mentioning a stalker I tracked down last year, and now Luc's son wants my help in finding this woman."

"Okay. Have you tried calling the FBI? Kidnapping is their territory."

"I was actually hoping you might have some intel on fine art forgery rings in my area." Iris now realized how presumptuous she sounded.

There was a long moment of silence, which gave Iris even more time to regret making this phone call.

"I'm not familiar with the New England networks. I guess I could ask my section chief for permission to do a little digging. We're not really supposed to do free-lance research."

"I'm sorry. I shouldn't have asked."

"It's okay. I'm out on horseback now, in the fields. No promises, but I'll call you back later if I can offer any useful information."

"Thanks so much, Kelly. I really appreciate this."

"Iris, do these people know you're looking for Luna Esposito?"

"They know Luna tried to call Ash, but I don't think they know about me."

"Good. Try to keep it that way. And tell Ash to lie low. These guys sound dangerous."

CHAPTER 41
THE PETRUCCI MOB

Iris finished the Friday dinner special Luc sent up for her to sample: sea bass with capers, roasted tomatoes and chervil— one of the perks of living with a chef. She was about to settle in on the living room sofa to start a new mystery novel when her phone buzzed.

"Hi, it's Kelly. I managed to get some information."

"Oh, God. Thank you so much. I hope I didn't get you in trouble."

"It's fine. I have an Interpol colleague on the East Coast who was intrigued by your request. He said there's been talk for years about the Petrucci mob family out of Providence, Rhode Island, having some artist on retainer to create forgeries. Every year a newly discovered Rodin, Pissarro, or Sisley was supposedly discovered in people's dusty attics. But this painter was so talented that no one could ever prove the paintings weren't real. Some low-level goombahs in the crime family tried to cut deals with the DA, offering tips about the guy, but it never led to finding him. Too much secrecy about his identity. Apparently, Marco Petrucci was the only one who dealt with him directly. The forger became a unicorn for my colleague, always out of reach. He was known as 'the Ghost'. Then, a few years ago, the trail went cold."

"That could be Luna's father! He died two or three years ago." Iris jotted down "Petrucci-Providence" on a scrap of paper.

"Maybe. If her father worked for that crime family, are you thinking Luna changed her identity to get away from them, then they found her and are forcing her to take over his work?"

That was exactly what Iris was thinking. "She's extremely talented in replicating late nineteenth-century paintings, right down to the crackling of the paint surface to age them. What if the Petruccis are holding Luna and her son as prisoners?"

"There's a kid involved? You need to contact the FBI! They deal with kidnappings and organized crime."

"But we don't know that it's the Petruccis who have them."

"You're right. Just because your young woman knows how to paint really well and there were rumors of a forger who might have been her father connected to a R.I. crime family won't be enough to convince the Feebees that the Petruccis have kidnapped her. Is Luna attractive? Maybe she was taken by someone to be trafficked. For the forgery angle to fly, you need more evidence."

Iris sat back and exhaled a long breath. She'd been trying to ignore the possibility of human trafficking as a cause for Luna's disappearance. Besides, it didn't fit the clues. "Any suggestions on how to verify if the Petrucci connection exists?"

Kelly was silent for a moment. "The old forger specialized in paintings from the late nineteenth century, right? My focus at Interpol is on stolen antiquities, so this isn't my field, but is there any specialized equipment or materials that a forger would need to buy to produce convincing works from that era?"

"I don't know, but I could try to find out. Are you thinking we could locate stores that sell supplies like that and track down the kidnappers through those sales? There's a Medford police detective looking into Luna's disappearance, although he's not making much progress. If I can figure out what to have him look for, the police could use their resources to check out art stores and online venders."

"I'm relieved to hear law enforcement is involved. If it is the Petrucci family who have Luna and her son, let the police move in on them. I'm serious, Iris. I know you're a badass, but this is the mob we may be talking about. These people are professional killers."

After Iris thanked Kelly for her help and rang off, she thought about particular materials that might be specific to that era of painting. She tried to recall technical details from the art history lectures she'd attended at Dartmouth, but nothing useful came to her. Maybe Ash would know.

Then she remembered she hadn't filled him in on her latest theory: that Luna might have been kidnapped for her forgery skills. She should call him. And Detective Stroud.

Iris drummed her fingers on the desk, excited by the possibility of puzzle pieces starting to fall into place. But she also heard Kelly's voice warning her about the danger of tangling with the Petruccis.

There were also Luc's fears to consider about getting entangled once again in life-threatening situations. She needed to bring him up to speed on these latest developments.

Was she drawn to the puzzle-solving aspects of this or to the danger itself? Wasn't the life she had—her work, her relationships—enough stimulation for her?

CHAPTER 42

MALIK-FRIDAY

Malik sat alone at the head of his large dining room table, savoring a bite of Dilara's crispy pork belly, neatly dipped in hot apple chutney. The meat was tender and juicy, just as his büyükanne used to make it years ago. Dilara was a marvelous find from his last trip to Turkey. That she could make the old recipes, spoke little English, and was happy to keep to herself in the basement maid's room, suited him just fine. Much better and cheaper than that gossipy Irish woman who'd commuted from Dorchester.

Malik sipped his rare red Grand Cru and considered the problem at hand. Over the last three days, Goran had discreetly trailed Ashley Burke and Iris Reid. None of their movements seemed too alarming until last night when Goran reported Burke had met with a cop at a diner. Malik shouldn't have been surprised. After a week and that aborted phone call, Burke had probably filed a missing person report. And Audrey Glenn mentioned the Reid woman knew Celia's old name. Still, they would never tie him to Celia. He'd made sure of that.

And then the damn pizza oven had been delayed. The restaurant supply store now promised they would deliver it first thing tomorrow morning, but that meant losing a day on an already tight schedule. Nonetheless, he hadn't bothered to go upstairs to check if the painting was done. He knew that by keeping Paul at the Nantucket house, Celia would be compliant. At any rate, Goran would watch her like a hawk during this last phase.

Malik scooped up some couscous with his fork and tasted it. Perfectly seasoned with just enough cumin and paprika.

He had already figured out how to get rid of Celia's body. But how could he stop Burke and Iris Reid from looking for her?

Malik took another sip of wine. If Celia's body was planted in a location where it was sure to be discovered, that would put an end to their search, wouldn't it? If not, the cleaners might need to arrange an accident.

CHAPTER 43

LUNA-FRIDAY

Luna waited nervously for Malik to appear, unsure what his mood would be after their confrontation the previous day. Now that she had corrected the boy's eyes, the painting was ready for the last phase: to be baked in an oven and glazed. She had waited all afternoon for his visit, but it was now after dinner, and he hadn't shown up. What did that mean?

Malik had been the one stressed about the painting being completely dry and ready to be returned to the owner in six more days. She'd need all that time for this last phase. Was he still waiting for the oven?

She wanted to be alert to her chance for escape during her time outside this room, but tonight, she was exhausted. Lying on her lumpy mattress on the floor, she watched the clouds float by through the grimy skylights in the sloped ceiling. It had been a week since she had slept longer than worried fits and starts. She tried not to panic about where Paul was and what might be happening to him. While the sleep deprivation numbed her, it also opened up room for other memories to intrude.

Luna's mother had died in childbirth, and her father raised her. His idea of childcare was to drag her playpen into his painting studio and sing to her while he worked. He had long white hair and a commanding voice. As a child, she had confused him with the God she heard about in Sunday School. She loved to watch him create beautiful images on canvas. Mysterious packages would arrive for Papa to unwrap, then the magic would begin.

"Come, let's see what we have here!" He would call to her before setting a new painting on the easel. "What do you think, *Stellina*, my little star? Is this artist any good? Bah—can Papa do a painting just as good?"

In grade school, Luna raced home each day, eager to check on the progress of his latest work. He'd describe each step in the process. In time, he let her paint alongside him, creating her own amateur copies—using a cheap canvas, mixing paints on a palette, scrutinizing the original artwork, then trying to imitate its brush strokes like Papa did.

She didn't need it spelled out that what they were doing was secret. She saw him paint any number of other boring still-lifes and seascapes to hang up around the house or sell through a touristy gallery in Newport, Rhode Island. But the special copies stayed in his basement studio under lock and key. And whenever someone came by to drop off or pick up one of those paintings, Papa made her hide in her room, out of sight.

In art class at school, she enjoyed drawing, creating collages, making things from clay, or using watercolors—anything but painting in oils. She knew instinctively to hide her facility in that medium, not to draw attention. Besides, by the time she got to high school, standing out for any particular talent was the last thing she wanted. She was far more interested in fitting in and attracting boys.

Luna was not, however, the type of girl that teenage boys

pursued. Aside from her glasses and frizzy red hair, she was shy, skinny, and flat-chested. But as she moved through her awkward teenage years, an amazing thing happened: her body and features began to co-operate, and she developed her own kind of ethereal beauty. Discovering hair-care products and contact lenses helped as well.

She gradually spent less time with her father and more time with her new boyfriend, Joey. They talked about getting away from her small town of Pawtucket in Rhode Island and moving to the big city of Boston or New York. Her father could stay here in their cottage, and she would visit him.

So, it was a surprise when one night at dinner, Papa's fork slipped to the floor. His hands were shaking. Luna picked up the fork. "What is wrong, Papa?"

He sighed heavily. "The doctor says it's Parkinson's. They ran tests for it yesterday. I've had symptoms for a while. I was going to tell you."

She had heard of the disease. A famous actor on TV had it, a neurodegenerative disease that slowly stole control of hands and limbs. "But how will you paint? That's your life. How long..."

"I don't know how long I have, but it's getting harder and harder to keep my hand steady. I'll need your help to finish this last copy before I quit for good. And we need to talk about your future. I want you to get away from the Petrucci family. Far away. Will you promise to do that?"

"Yes, Papa. But you must come with me."

CHAPTER 44
A COOL TRICK

Iris thought about her conversation with Kelly as she carried her dinner plate to the kitchen and loaded it into the dishwasher. How was she supposed to find out if someone had bought specialized equipment or the other materials needed to create fake Old Master paintings? And what if they didn't need to buy supplies because they were already stocked up? Still, it was worth a shot.

Standing in front of the open refrigerator, she stared at the inviting bottle of Riesling. Better not. She should keep a clear head.

Hold on. What's-her-name taught that course at the art academy on late nineteenth century painting. Audrey Glenn. Iris could ask her. She consulted her watch. It was late on a Friday night to be phoning a near-stranger. But what about Zane and Kiara? They'd taken Glenn's class, and kids their age wouldn't mind being called at this hour.

Iris went to her phone's call history and redialed a number she thought was Zane's. She recognized Kiara's voice answering.

"Hi, it's Iris Reid again. You got a minute for a question?" She heard loud rock blaring, before it was suddenly turned down.

"Did you find Celia?"

"Not yet, but we're still looking for her. Could I ask you something technical from Audrey Glen's class?"

After Iris got more specific, Kiara shrieked, "Hey—are you gonna paint a forgery?"

"No-o-o. This is for an article I'm writing." Had she ever mentioned what she did for a living?

Kiara consulted with someone in the background before coming back on the line. "Okay, here's something. The painters back then used white lead paint, which is toxic. But in the twentieth century, they switched to titanium white paint with no lead. It was healthier, but lead paint, called flake white, produces a warmer, less chalky tone. Appraisers can test for lead paint, so if you're trying to forge a nineteenth-century painting, you can't use titanium white. Is that the kind of thing you want to know?"

"Yeah, exactly. Do art supply stores still sell lead flake white paint?"

"Only a few stores stock it, mainly for conservators. The pigment they used to make flake paint is scarce and really expensive. This is for an article? Like for a blog?"

"Right. It's for *Art Through the Ages*," Iris improvised.

"Hmm. Never heard of it."

Iris sat back. Did she finally have an actionable clue? *Maybe Kiara knew more.* "How do you age a canvas to get that crackled look?"

"Actually, Celia taught us this cool trick." Kiara's voice was animated. "You need to bake the painting in a big oven, then varnish it between each turn. It takes days because the canvas needs time to dry in between. Celia used the technique on the final project she did for Ms. Glenn's class. Her canvas was too large to fit in a regular oven, so she convinced the pizza place down the street to let her use their oven after hours. It really blew Ms. Glenn's mind when she saw it. And even the snotty art appraiser who came to our critique was impressed. He tried to hide it, but his eyes almost popped out of his head when he looked at it closely."

"Could you use anything else to apply the heat? Maybe a hairdryer or a heat lamp?" Iris asked.

"I don't think so. Celia said it was a tricky process, and you could screw it up if you didn't get the low heat applied evenly across the whole canvas."

"How long did it take Celia to make the painting for your final class project?"

"Ms. Glenn only gave us two weeks. Celia's project was definitely the most elaborate. But she can paint super-fast, even with the baking part taking five or six days."

"The baking takes five or six days?" Iris repeated.

"Yeah. You need to wait for it to dry between sessions." Iris heard someone speaking indistinctly to Kiara on the other end. "I've gotta go. I hope that's useful for your blog. Let me know if you find Celia."

"Definitely, thanks." Iris now had two potential leads. She needed to tell Ash.

She punched in his number, but the connection went directly to voicemail. He must be working.

Call me, she texted.

Then she remembered Ellie saying Raven was driving up from Providence on Saturday to stay with Ash. Iris assumed he was planning to break up with her then. She felt profoundly sad at the thought of her goddaughter going through such heartbreak. After Iris learned officially that the couple were no longer together, she'd ask Ellie if there was some way she could comfort Raven, maybe take her on a trip, just the two of them.

Before turning in for the night, she decided to leave a voicemail for Detective Stroud. Maybe he could get his tech team started early Saturday morning to check for sales of pizza ovens and flake white paint.

Finally, it felt like they'd picked up Luna's trail! Iris didn't want to lose another minute to find out where it led. If Luna could produce a convincing forgery in two weeks, time was running out.

CHAPTER 45

MALIK-SATURDAY

At seven a.m. on Saturday morning, Malik stared at the monster cardboard container on his front stoop. *Where the hell am I supposed to put this thing?* Three beefy guys from the downtown kitchen supply store looked at him expectantly as snow collected on their caps and jackets. Malik motioned them to bring the box inside and rest it on the marble foyer floor while he considered what to do.

He had paid little attention to the oven's specifications when Celia chose it from a catalog. He'd imagined it fitting in Celia's studio space upstairs. "Can this be plugged into a regular outlet?" he thought to ask the tall delivery man with acne-scarred cheeks, who had a patch on his jacket reading "Fred."

"No way," Fred said. "You got a dryer? Those have the 220-volt plug you need."

Fred glanced around the entry hall at the crystal chandelier and antique table. "Gotta ask, why do you even need a commercial pizza oven?"

Malik thought fast. "My kids come on weekends and love my homemade pizzas."

"They make smaller versions of these big boys," Fred said.

"I have a lot of kids," Malik snapped, then came to a decision. "Bring it down to the laundry room in the basement. The door's over there."

Fred pulled a tape measure out of his pocket and scoped out the narrow staircase. He compared the box's size to the width and turning radius of the stairs before shaking his head. "We'll have to unpack it here. The box is too big."

Even after the wood straps, Styrofoam packing, and cardboard were removed, the oven barely made it to the basement. Malik assumed it needed to be that large to fit the painting inside.

As the men jockeyed their load down to the laundry room, Malik followed them. He surveyed the space, not a room he'd visited often. It spanned the front third of the house, with a maid's room and his studio in back, half a level below the sidewalk.

The thought of the devious Celia moving from the attic down all the way through the townhouse to reach the basement made him nervous. He studied the laundry room for possible exits. Its only two windows were secured with ornate wrought iron grates, but there was a door under the front staircase which led up to the sidewalk next to Louisburg Square. The door was locked, but even so, Malik would warn Goran to watch the artist's every move.

Fred and his helpers shimmied the heavy appliance into position next to the dryer and plugged it in. He looked over his shoulder at Malik. "These things gotta be vented, ya know. Want me to attach it to the dryer vent?"

Malik waved his hand in a go-ahead gesture. Ten minutes later, he escorted them out, slipping Fred and his men several big bills.

Now that the oven was hooked up, he needed to get Celia

started today. They were cutting it close. The copy had to be finished and completely dry by next Friday.

What were the chances, with her son out of reach, that Celia would make a run for it in the next few days? Would she consciously leave her son behind to fend for himself?

CHAPTER 46

THE LOVE OF MY LIFE

Ash woke up Saturday morning with a heavy weight on his chest. Literally. Kevin sat there, staring down intently, willing him to open his eyes.

He shoved the cat off him. "You'll get fed when I get up. The vet said you're supposed to be on a diet." His phone, propped up on a table by the bed, read nine a.m. Ash remembered staying up most of the night painting. He pulled a pillow over his head. Today was going to be intense. He'd arranged for Raven to come by at noon for "an important discussion." Ash owed it to her to break up in person, however much he was dreading seeing her upset.

Twenty minutes later, he climbed groggily out of bed and lumbered over to the kitchenette to make coffee. As the water in the espresso pot on the stove started to bubble, his cell phone buzzed, displaying an unknown number.

"Uh-huh?" he croaked.

"It's Detective Stroud. Did I wake you, Ashley?"

"Is this about Luna? Did you find her?"

"Not yet, but I got Basia Sobieski's burner phone out of

185

Evidence. If you want, we can try your idea of calling the number found on her phone to see if it rings somewhere in Luna's apartment. That's assuming the battery hasn't run down. Who knows? It might have other relevant phone numbers on it."

"Okay, yeah, great. Give me half-an-hour to get ready, then hit the intercom for my studio. I'll let you in."

After mainlining several espressos and feeding Kevin, Ash took a shower and pulled on black jeans and Bob Marley T-shirt from the night before. He was frowning at the canvas he'd been working on, thinking it needed more depth, more shadows, more something, when the buzzer rang.

Detective Stroud carried Basia's phone in a plastic evidence bag as he followed Ash across the hall into Luna's studio. The room still smelled slightly of turpentine, paint, and a whiff of her scent. Ash walked over to a small worktable and picked up one of her sable brushes, looking at it sadly. "Is there a redial button on that thing?"

"It's not that simple. We had to get the call detail records from the cellular carrier. They keep a log history on all phones, even burners. Since the phone's owner was murdered, we didn't need a warrant." Stroud took a notebook out of his jacket pocket. "Why don't you stand at the other end of the room, and I'll cover this side. See if we can hear anything. Ready?"

He waited near the bathroom door as Stroud punched in the only digits found on Basia's call history.

Ash thought he could detect a faint ringing, or was he imagining it? He and Stroud both walked slowly and softly toward the daybed. A muted tone pulsated from under the bed. Ash crouched down and swept the dusty floor under the bedsprings with his phone's flashlight. In a corner, he found a small case. Retrieving it, he flipped open the flap, and a phone fell out onto the bed.

"Hey—it worked!" Ash laughed. "Now what do we do?"

"Don't touch it. There might be prints on it." Stroud approached and, with his own phone, photographed it lying next to a pillow. He retrieved a pair of nitrile gloves from his jacket pocket and slipped them on, dropping Luna's phone into a new evidence bag. "To get the call history for this one, I will need a warrant. But given the circumstances, that shouldn't be too hard. It's the weekend, but we might hear back from the cell carrier by Tuesday if we're lucky."

"And that will tell us who Luna called or who called her on this burner, right?"

"Yeah, but assuming Luna was the one who bought both of the burners in order to communicate with Basia Sobieski, it's doubtful that the kidnappers' phone number will be on here. Unless they got Ms. Sobieski to reveal Luna's phone number before they killed her. If Luna had seen a call coming from Sobieski's phone, she would have answered it, and they could have threatened to hurt the boy if she didn't come to meet them. If nothing else, it can verify the connection between the two women."

Ash remained seated on the daybed. "What else can we do? I can't stand waiting around, imagining what she might be going through."

"With the information you gave me yesterday, I now have several divisions working on this. We're trying to track down information about Luna's father and to find Paul's birth certificate. If the boy's father is named on it, he might be able to shed some light on who Luna was hiding from."

Ash grimaced at this mention of Paul's father, and Stroud looked at him curiously. "Can I ask you something? What is Luna Esposito to you? You said she was a friend, but I get the feeling there's more to it than that."

Ash offered the detective a sad smile and sighed. "I think Luna might just be the love of my life."

They both turned at the creak of the entry door. Raven stood in the doorway, her eyes wide and her mouth hanging open.

CHAPTER 47

LA-DI-DA

I ris found herself on Saturday morning in an otherwise-empty bed. She called out, "Luc?"

Getting no answer, she threw on her robe and headed to the kitchen. A small Japanese bowl weighed down a note on the counter. "Need to meet a new supplier at the farmer's market. Sorry, babe. Want me to reserve you a table at the restaurant tonight?"

Missing out on Luc's company on Friday and Saturday evenings was one thing, and par for the course with a chef for a boyfriend, but Saturday and Sunday mornings were their time for lolling in bed. It was sacrosanct, or at least it had been. Iris crumpled the note and angrily threw it in the trash.

As Sheba waited attentively, Iris filled the dog's bowl with kibble, cutting up some pieces of chicken to put on top. Yawning, she turned on the industrial-strength espresso machine and waited for the familiar hissing and thumping noises to cycle through.

By the time she had finished two cappuccinos and done all of the games in *the New York Times* including the crossword puzzle, her phone vibrated on the counter, slowly dancing itself in a circle. Once she saw the display: Det. Stroud, she picked it up.

"Ms. Reid. I hope I'm not interrupting your Saturday."

Unfortunately not. "Thanks for calling. You got my message from last night?"

"That's why I rang. I gave your leads to our tech crew last night, and they ran them through their databases. We compared the receipts from art stores that carried the special type of leaded paint and a bunch of restaurant supply outlets. Then we cross-referenced the two lists. This morning, we got a few interesting hits. Most pizza ovens were sold to restaurants, which typically had certain tax exemption tags. Only two ovens were sold in the last few weeks to residences. One went to a big spread out in Weston where it was specified by a decorator for a fancy outdoor kitchen. The other was delivered to a townhouse in Beacon Hill this morning. The owner of the supply house said he delivered it personally."

"Beacon Hill? Basia Sobieski was driving a car with a Beacon Hill Resident parking sticker on it."

"The restaurant supply owner said it struck him as odd that the owner wanted the pizza oven installed in the laundry room in the basement. It was like the guy hadn't thought it out beforehand how he was going to actually use it."

Iris tried to control her breathing. "You said the techs cross-referenced oven sales with purchases of white flake paint? Did this Beacon Hill guy purchase that as well?"

"Yes, within Massachusetts and Rhode Island, there were five tubes of old-style flake white paint sold in the last few months. The Beacon Hill resident bought two of them ten days ago. But another artist on the Cape purchased the other three tubes a month ago."

"The Beacon Hill guy's got to be the one who has Luna! What's his name? Where does he live?"

"Hold on. We can't jump to conclusions. This guy, Malik Saban, is a hotshot art appraiser and works with all the big auction houses in Boston and New York. A lot of rich art collectors bring their paintings to him to verify that they're not fakes. Mr. Saban is wealthy and well-connected. For a judge to give us a warrant to look inside his townhouse, we'd need more than the fact that he bought a pizza oven and some white leaded paint. He could claim that he intended to move the oven outside in the warmer months for entertaining. And Saban might use the paint for legitimate restoration work. Judges want to see convincing evidence of a crime."

"Detective Stroud, no disrespect, but would you hesitate to investigate Mr. Saban if he weren't rich and well-connected? Luna and her son may not have much time left. Once the painter is at the baking and varnishing stage, I've learned it takes only five or six days until the forgery is done. After that, Malik Saban may have no further use for either of them."

CHAPTER 48
BULLFINCH

After ending the call with the detective, Iris opened her laptop on the dining table and typed Malik Saban into the browser. The photo on his polished website showed a good-looking man, fiftyish, with dark hair graying at the temples. His patrician features reminded Iris of her brother, Sterling. The services the site offered were for fine art authentication in his state-of-the art workshop, using the most stringent methods in the industry. Iris figured it was targeted at high-profile institutions and individuals, with consultations available by appointment only. The contact button listed no address or phone number, only an email link.

Iris went back to the browser and, with a few clicks, was able to locate Saban's address on Louisburg Square in Beacon Hill. *Well, la-di-da. The most expensive real estate in the city.* Is that where Luna and Paul were being held prisoner? She assumed this meant they weren't in some grubby basement. Or was she jumping too quickly to conclusions, making connections based only on guesswork?

But something Kiara had said popped into her head: a snotty art appraiser was at their final Audrey Glenn critique, and Luna's copy of the Monet painting had impressed him. That could have been where Malik Saban first encountered her. An appraiser who took in valuable art pieces would be the perfect cover for scams quietly switching out forgeries for originals.

By now, it was noon, late enough on a weekend to call Kiara.

An irritated female voice answered. "Mmmm?"

"Sorry, it's Iris Reid again with one quick question. Was Malik Saban the name of the art appraiser who came to your final crit for Audrey Glenn's class?"

"Maybe. Wait. Let me ask Zane." Iris heard muffled background sounds before Kiara came back on. "Yeah, Zane says that was the guy."

"Thanks. Sorry to bother you."

It looked like a strong possibility that Saban was the guy keeping Luna and Paul captive. Iris rubbed the back of her neck. But if Detective Stroud was unwilling to even get a warrant to search 23 Louisburg Square, how could Iris convince the police to go rescue her? Iris needed to get proof.

The detective had said the pizza oven was installed in the basement laundry room that morning. Assuming Luna was the one overseeing the final stages of baking and varnishing, that meant she would need to be in the basement for periods of time over the next few days. This might be their only chance of getting to her.

Iris went to her bedroom to get dressed. As she layered on a thermal shirt, heavy sweater, and wool pants, she wondered what was going on with Raven and Ash. Was it ridiculous to hope that they had somehow worked things out? Iris knew from sad experience that you couldn't force someone to love you just because you loved them.

When she returned to her laptop on the dining room table, she had an idea. She found the website of the Boston Inspectional

Services Department. While the office would be closed on a weekend, information about properties in the city was generally available on its site, depending on how up to date the system was.

Iris plugged in *23 Louisburg Square* and waited. The building
jacket contained all permits applied for since the ISD was estab-
lished in 1981, as well as older scanned materials. Iris flipped
through the offerings, from delicate hand-drawn floor plans and
elevations from the previous two centuries to modern Computer-
Aided-Design drawings. Saban's impressive Greek Revival townhouse had been built in 1842 by Charles Bullfinch! Wow—Bullfinch
was architectural royalty in Boston.

She studied a street-front elevation drawn in 1922, submitted by
an architect requesting permission from the historic commission to
change the height of the handrail at the front stoop. Iris was
focused on how she could approach one of the laundry room
windows to take a photo of Luna to show Detective Stroud. A
leaded-glass fanlight and two sidelights flanked the substantial
main door on the elevated first floor. The tops of two basement
windows showed on the drawing just above ground level, with the
bottoms of them dotted in. Stairs appeared to lead under the front
staircase to what was probably a basement door, often secured
behind a locked wrought-iron gate.

Accompanying drawings showed the rear view of the basement
elevation dotted in as being completely underground with two rear
window wells allowing light to enter. The backyard was shown
level with the first floor. Wedging herself down into one of those
wells might work if they were roomy enough, assuming nothing
else had changed since the previous century. But if she remembered
right, the backyards of those houses had no access to the street.
They were completely landlocked.

After studying these old drawings to judge the townhouse's
exterior, Iris flipped through the rest of the records until she found

floor plans showing the layout of interior rooms. The 1922 plan showed an old-fashioned basement kitchen that looked designed for servants to use. Iris knew that, in the modern era, most of these old Georgian cook's kitchens had been moved to the first floor to become family gathering spots. She needed to find more recent floor plans to confirm the current configuration. And where was Saban's "cutting-edge workshop" touted on his website? Why didn't they arrange these damn records in chronological order?

Iris eventually found a set of drawings from the 1970s showing that the kitchen had indeed been moved to the first floor, and a laundry room was now located in the front section of the basement. Bingo. That's where Luna would be working. Two rooms, one labeled storage and the other called a maid's room, took up the rear floor space. One or both of those back rooms could now be the workshop.

This begged the question: how many people now lived and worked in this townhouse? No partner or spouse had shown up when Iris had checked Malik Saban's name on a people searching site. Given that the real estate webpages valued this property at around twenty million dollars, how much staff did Saban employ to run this place? Besides a housekeeper and a cook, he would need guards for Luna and Paul. Maybe a nanny for the boy. Did they all live in the building?

And what kind of security system would Saban have? Probably something discrete and state-of-the-art with cameras. She wasn't going to be able to creep up to the basement windows to get proof of Luna's location for the police. Could she use a telephoto lens from a car window? Probably not, and she didn't own one of those anyway. The zoom setting on her phone would have to do.

Iris stood up and paced around her spacious living room. She'd come so far with this search, being pretty sure she knew where Luna was being held, and why. And the drawings of the building showed the room in which Luna would likely be working. They also showed the windows through which Iris needed to get photographs without tripping off the security system. As an architect, she should be able to figure how to accomplish that. Designing ways into and out of buildings was part of her training.

She let out a scream of frustration. Why was she doing this alone?

She needed to call Ash.

CHAPTER 49

A DOG IN A PLAID COAT

This time when Iris called Ash, he picked up. There was traffic noise in the background.

"Hey, Iris. I'm in the car heading back from Providence." He sounded exhausted. "Can I call you back when I get home?"

Providence? He must have been with Raven. Was that a good sign or a bad one? Should she even mention Luna now? "Everything okay?"

"Not really, and I can't talk about it. I didn't get any sleep last night, and I'm really beat. I'm gonna go home and rest, then I'll call you, okay?"

"Sure. Drive carefully. We can catch up later."

She ended the call. Damn. Ash didn't have the bandwidth to deal with this, and Detective Stroud wanted proof before the police would take the next step. But Luna and Paul could be running out of time.

SHEBA, UNHAPPILY BUNDLED UP IN A BUFFALO PLAID COAT, SAT IN HER dog seat in the back of the car as Iris parallel parked in a rare open spot on Charles Street. What could be more innocent than a woman walking her well-dressed dog around Louisburg Square, admiring the classic architecture? Iris helped the low-slung hound down to the curb and snapped on her leash. She pulled her knit cap low on her forehead and retrieved a pair of sunglasses from her pocket.

They ambled up Pinckney Street for two blocks, past the elegant, attached townhouses. Iris looked for an alley that might cut in to the backyards of the Louisburg Square houses but reached the small, enclosed park without seeing any openings between buildings. She tugged slightly on Sheba's leash to start them on a slow circuit around the square, while taking photos with her phone of the stately brick houses with their black shutters. She heard the screech of a Mercedes station wagon scraping a high granite curb nearby as its driver parked and a heavy front door clicked open and then slammed shut on the far side of the park. Iris knew Malik's property was five buildings along, so she slowed down as she and the dog approached it. As she had noted on the building department drawings, the ground sloped enough here for the first floor to be elevated a half story. The two basement windows were protected by wrought-iron grates, and an ornamental but beefy-looking iron gate stood between the archway under the stairs and the basement door behind. No one would get through those barriers easily.

"Time to poop." She nudged her dog over toward a tree on the sidewalk directly outside Malik's basement windows. Sheba sniffed at the nasty bare dirt surrounding the tree, then crouched. Iris made a show of taking a poop bag out of her pocket, stretching it over her hand and stooping, ready to do her dog-owner duty. As Iris waited, she peered into one of the basement windows five feet away. No one was visible inside, but she thought she could see a washing machine with a dryer pulled away from the wall at an angle. She bent down to collect Sheba's deposit and angled closer to the window to photograph the shadowy object next to the dryer.

As soon as she took one picture, a mechanical whirring sound diverted her attention over to the exterior staircase. A wall-mounted security camera was rotating to face her. Iris hurried back to the sidewalk. She retreated as casually as she could to Mount Vernon Street, not daring to look back and check if anyone was pursuing her.

Her heart didn't stop thudding until she and Sheba were back at the car. Her fingers fumbled as she snapped Sheba into her car harness and locked herself inside the driver's seat.

Had anyone spotted her snooping?

CHAPTER 50
MALIK-SATURDAY

Malik leaned back in his desk chair in the basement workshop. He had listed in his Hermès green alligator phone directory the contact number he wanted under "cleaners," an inside joke. He punched in the digits.

"I'd like to reserve a package pickup for Friday evening, on the late side. Let's say 10 p.m. Yes, the package will be wrapped, but you'll be doing the finishing and disposal. I'll let you know on Friday where the package should be sent. I'm at 23 Louisburg Square, Boston—the Saban account. Oh, there's an outside chance I might need it picked up a few days earlier. Would that be a problem? Good. I'll wire the usual payment. Thank you."

Always a pleasure dealing with professionals. Celia had finished the painting on Friday, and he had it in front of him now. It looked fantastic. Other than the crackling, it could fool anyone. She'd start the final baking and varnishing stage that evening, and it should take no more than five days. If she misbehaved before the aging was complete, Malik would study her technique and finish the damned forgery himself. He wanted her gone. He couldn't trust her. Too bad though to lose such a talented forger.

The client was returning from Geneva this week and stopping by on Saturday to pick up his "original" Sargent after its appraisal. Malik had every intention of returning it with the happy news that, although it was a lesser-known Sargent portrait, it was absolutely authentic.

Should he let Celia see Paul one last time? He wasn't heartless. But no, that might be harder for the boy. He had to think about Paul's future welfare. Let him gradually forget about the mother. Helen can bring him back from Nantucket after Celia has been disposed of. Malik would explain to Paul his mother had died, which would be true.

Malik walked over to his workbench and turned off the spectroscope he had been using to analyze the pigments in the Sargent copy. He needed to make sure that it could pass any future tests. This week, he would keep Celia's painting along with the original in his locked room, to be handed over to Celia only when she was actively working on this last stage. He couldn't risk her damaging either canvas in an attempt at revenge.

Malik lifted the original Sargent from the table and walked over to a bookcase along the far wall. He shoved aside several large art books to reveal a small panel. Fingers tapping quickly on the keypad, he stepped back as a section of the bookcase swung open and he entered a small room. After flipping on the lights, he closed the bookcase door behind him. The temperature and humidity control system made a low, reassuring hum. He switched off the alarm and checked the thermostat to make sure that it remained at a constant sixty-eight degrees.

Four easels stood in a semicircle, one of them empty. A spotlight carefully illuminated each position. He lifted the Sargent onto the remaining mount and stood back to study the effect.

A Georges Seurat, a J.M.W. Turner, and a Mary Cassatt—those were the original paintings he had kept, all smaller canvases than the Sargent. Unfortunately, he'd previously had to sell a Rubens and a Marcel Duchamp to support his lifestyle. The choice of artwork that was brought to him for authentication circumscribed his choices for this collection. Malik returned most pieces to their museums or owners intact so as not to arouse suspicion.

Now, he had to decide which of the other three he would sell if he wanted to keep the Sargent. He paused in front of the Seurat landscape with its flickering surface of tiny dots. Classic Pointillism, but did the subject grab him emotionally? From there to the Turner he'd acquired several years ago—a sunset over a violent sea. He took in its brilliant brushwork, evoking pure light with Turner's signature use of shimmering color. This one spoke to him intellectually. He would hang on to it. He moved on to Mary Cassatt's *Woman in a Bonnet*. It was a first-rate example of Impressionism, even if the figure looked a bit flat to him. Still, he would keep this one as well for the collection. He'd part with the Seurat. There was a big black market in Switzerland for the Pointillists. Something about all that anal precision.

Malik turned to his newest prize and sighed. He moved closer to admire how Sargent had masterfully rendered the boy's rosy flesh tones. He felt bewitched by the boy's soulful gaze. The painting spoke to every bit of him. He would never part with this one.

CHAPTER 51
THE SABAN ACCOUNT

At four that afternoon, Ash's phone alarm beeped relentlessly until he finally rolled over and smacked it silent. He lay in bed in the sun-filled room, trying to recall why he was sleeping in his clothes in the middle of the day. Then the last five hours came roaring back to him. Raven arriving early and overhearing him talk about his feelings for Luna. Chasing Raven back to her apartment in Providence to try to soften the blow. Seeing her so hurt while still longing for Luna. Shit! He was a bad person.

Ash staggered to the kitchen to make himself coffee and noticed Kevin lying in his usual spot by the front door, looking forlorn.

"I miss her too, buddy." Would either of them ever see Luna again?

Ash sat on a stool at his worktable, nursing his coffee, trying to fully awaken his brain. His phone showed several missed calls from Iris last night and this morning. He called her back.

"Sorry I've been out of commission," he said. "Have you made any progress?"

"You could say that." Iris spent the next fifteen minutes walking Ash through all the discoveries. She explained how her Interpol friend had led her to suspect Luna's father of being a forger mixed up with the Petrucci mob family in Providence. Luna's friends had told them about an art appraiser who'd noticed Luna's skill while critiquing her Audrey Glenn project. And Detective Stroud had cross-referenced the forgery materials. Checking two sets of store receipts had led back to this very same art appraiser, who was probably holding Luna in his Beacon Hill townhouse to copy artwork. But Iris warned Ash they needed proof that Luna was inside before the police would ask for a warrant to enter the town-house and rescue her.

Ash stood up so fast he knocked over his coffee cup. "Luna's alive? And just across the river in Boston? We have to go get her! I'll break the door down!"

"Wait. I went there already today to scope it out. There are cameras and a serious alarm system. These might be the people who killed Basia Sobieski. If we tried forcing our way in, we'd probably end up dead as well. I don't know if they're part of Petrucci's network or a different operation."

"But this guy could kill her at any time. We have to do something!"

"I have an idea. Why don't you come to the loft, and I'll drive us over to Beacon Hill. And Ash..."

"Yeah?"

"Wear black."

CHAPTER 52
LORD OF THE FRIES

I n the late afternoon, Iris drove past 23 Louisburg Square. She and Ash looked for any lights or activity in the basement. There was nothing.

"It's probably better if we come back after dark." Iris double-parked and checked the weather app on her phone. "Sunset's at 5:30. We have half an hour or so to wait."

She drove down Mount Vernon Street to the flat of Beacon Hill and wedged her car into a semi-legal spot on River Street, a few blocks away. Iris led Ash around the corner to the Lord of the Fries restaurant, a low-key neighborhood institution.

"Let's grab an early dinner and use their restroom. We may have a long night ahead waiting to spot Luna." Iris remembered descriptions of P.I.s or cops on surveillance having to pee in bottles so as not to leave their vantage points. She drew the line at that much dedication to their mission.

Ash looked skeptical as he scanned the menu in the window, then brightened. "They actually have some vegan options."

At this early hour, they were seated right away at a table across from an open kitchen. A waiter took their order: quinoa salad for Ash and ragu Bolognese for Iris. While they waited for their food, she showed him the picture she'd taken earlier of the townhouse, enlarging the one taken through the laundry room window. "That looks like a pizza oven, doesn't it?"

Ash squinted at her phone screen. "It's hard to make out." He studied the wrought-iron security grates over the windows and the door under the stairway, then handed Iris back her phone. "What's the plan? If we see Luna inside, how are we going to get her out? And what about her kid?"

"Think of this as reconnaissance. We need to know how well they are guarding her and what the household schedule is. We can try to get some pictures of her to show Detective Stroud. That would have to be enough proof for a warrant. And maybe we can somehow signal her. If she knows we've found her, it will give her hope."

Ash raked his hair back with both hands. "She's got to be there, right?"

Iris sidestepped the question. "These are the best leads we have."

The waiter brought their dinner, and Iris ate absently, her mind on their mission ahead. Ash seemed equally distracted. As soon as his plate was empty, he wadded up his napkin and leaned back in his chair. "Your friend from Interpol said Luna grew up in some Rhode Island mob family?"

Iris signaled the waiter for the check before answering. "Interpol has been trying for years to track down an expert painter the Petrucci crime family in Providence was using to forge Old Masters. It might have been her father. He was known as "the Ghost." Some lower-level wise guys offered tips on where he lived, but these never panned out. Then Interpol lost the forger's trail several years ago."

"When her father died," Ash said.

"If 'the Ghost' was her father, that doesn't mean he willingly cooperated with the Petruccis."

Ash raised an eyebrow.

"Or that Luna had anything to do with the racket," Iris said. "Just because her father taught her how to paint doesn't mean she was planning to take over this hypothetical operation forging for the Mob."

Iris looked over at the waiter. She was dying for a cup of coffee, but the thought of no bathroom access for the next few hours killed that desire. She grabbed the check just as Ash reached for it. "Don't forget, Luna left her hometown and moved to Boston for art school. She may have been trying to hide from the Petruccis."

"Then she gets swept up by another bad guy who wants to cash in on her artistic skills."

"Kiara said the painting Luna did for Audrey Glenn's class was totally different from the more abstract work she had been doing. Maybe she'd been trying to hide her more traditional painting facility so as not to attract attention."

"That might make her current 'Prisoners' series, with figures hidden behind veils of paint, a statement about shielding that side of her talent."

"Or about having to hide her identity behind veils."

Iris added the tip, signed the bill, and put her credit card back in her wallet. "Like a cry for help, maybe."

They bundled back up in their coats, hats and scarves, and headed out into the chilly night toward the car.

The parking options around Louisburg Square were limited. They needed good sight lines into Malik's basement. Most of the reserved residents spots were filled. The lights on Malik's first floor were now brightly lit, but the house next door was in darkness, other than a single front porch light. Iris decided to take a chance that the neighbors were away on vacation, no doubt off in Aspen or Harbour Island for a winter break, and she could borrow their parking space. If they showed up, she'd play the clueless tourist and move.

She parked carefully and shut off the engine. "We can start the car up again when we get cold." She and Ash trained their binoculars on the tall first-floor windows, hoping to see some movement, but the curtains in the narrow openings between the drapes were opaque.

After a silent twenty minutes sitting side by side in the dark car, Iris was tempted to ask Ash how things had gone with Raven but decided not to increase the tension already present. "Want to listen to some music?"

Ash reached into his pocket and held up AirPods. "Good idea. I'll use these, so you can put on whatever you want to listen to."

Iris heard the beat of loud electronic rap escaping from around Ash's earbuds. She turned the car radio on low to an alternative rock station playing *Boygenius*.

Her phone pinged with a text. Iris gripped it tighter when she saw it was from Ellie.

< Ash broke up with Raven. She's beside herself. I'm going down to Providence to be with her. >

She texted back:

< I'm so sorry. Send her my love and a big hug. Let's talk when you get back. >

Iris rubbed her temples. *Could Ellie tell that she already knew about this? But she couldn't have betrayed Ash's confidence. Was it disloyal to her goddaughter to be helping Ash find this woman?* Her head felt like it was in a vise.

Iris slid her phone back into her pocket. She'd figure out what to say to Ellie and Raven after this night was over.

Suddenly, Ash sat up tall. "Look, a light in the basement!"

His words pulled Iris from her thoughts. She brought her binoculars to her eyes and saw a bald man walking over to what she figured was the pizza oven. He bent over and fiddled with something before turning and leaving the room.

"Bet he just turned the oven on. It will need time to preheat."

"Then we should see Luna!" Ash laughed nervously.

Unless I've misjudged all the clues, Iris thought.

Ten minutes later, Iris noticed steam coming out of a vent next to one of the basement windows. "See that condensation by the window? They must have hooked up the oven to the old dryer vent."

"Is that significant?"

"Maybe." Her headache was compounded by her focusing so hard on the narrow rectangle of light that was the basement window. She consciously unclenched her jaw, took a sip from her water bottle, and tried to concentrate on breathing.

The door on the far side of the laundry room swung open again.

A man Iris recognized as Malik Saban entered holding a framed painting. He laid it down carefully on top of the washing machine, then left the room.

"That's Malik Saban, the art appraiser." Iris explained.

"Bastard!" Ash said under his breath.

A few moments later, Malik reappeared holding a second painting of the same size, this one unframed. He placed this on a small table near the window. Iris could make out the man's features as he peered down at the picture.

Ash was frozen in place, eyes glued to his binoculars. She heard him suck in a breath. Iris looked past him, and there she was, being led into the room by the bald man clutching her by the arm.

Luna Esposito at last.

CHAPTER 53
GO NOW!

Luna's appearance shocked Iris. In the week she'd been gone, the poor woman looked like she'd lost ten pounds and aged ten years. Her face was haggard, and her clothes looked filthy.

Ash moaned in distress. He turned to Iris. "What have they done to her? I need to do something. Should I take a photo of her to send to Stroud? Maybe he can get her out of there tonight."

"Wait. Malik and the guard are both in the room with her, and you don't want to attract their attention. They might hurt her. Or Paul. Also, there's a camera attached on the side of the front staircase. It rotates to follow any motion it senses. Probably has night vision as well. We don't know who might be monitoring it."

One of the gas streetlights common across Beacon Hill was near the edge of Malik's property. If Ash was on the sidewalk, its light would be behind him, leaving his face in shadow. Still, any outside noise might cause the men inside to startle and behave unpredictably.

"So how should I do this?"

"Get your phone's camera ready before you get out of the car. Set it to zoom in. You'll only have a few seconds to get a photo or two before they notice you. Then walk slowly back to the car. We can text the shot to Stroud and see what he says."

"Right." Ash began tapping on his phone to set it up.

As Luna walked over to look at the unframed painting, Malik turned and left the room.

"Go now!" Iris gave Ash's shoulder a nudge. "Slow and steady!"

But just as Ash approached the window and swung the phone up to his eye, Malik reentered the room holding paintbrushes and a can of something. He faced Ash directly. Luna followed his gaze out the window.

Iris couldn't tell what Malik or Luna could actually see, but Luna's captor rushed over to the windows and yanked the drapes closed.

Breathing heavily, Ash returned to the passenger seat and gently closed the car door. "Holy shit! Did he see me?"

"He must have seen something. Did you get a photo?"

"I took two before he closed the curtains."

Iris and Ash hunched over his phone, then both swore. The two shots were blurry. You could make out a woman near the window with a man behind her but given Luna's changed appearance and the poor quality of the shots, identification wasn't a sure thing.

"I'll send these to Stroud anyway," Iris said. "Maybe his techs can sharpen the images." She found the detective's contact number and texted him, explaining where they were and what they had just seen.

Ash rested his head against the side window. "I can't believe I screwed this up." His eyes darted nervously to the front door. "Do you think Malik's going to come out here and look for me?"

"No, I doubt he could see what you were doing. You could have been a pedestrian passing by. But now that the curtains are closed, I'm not sure what else we can do. Between the security system and the two guys guarding Luna, I don't know any way to get to her. We'll have to wait for the police to get a warrant." She hoped Ash hadn't noticed the gun holster inside the bald guy's jacket.

Iris' phone pinged with a text. Stroud wrote:

< You shouldn't be there. Leave this to us. I'll see what we can do with these photos and try to get a warrant tomorrow. Go home! >

After reading it, Ash clenched his fist. "Luna can't afford to wait! Did you see her? God knows what they've done to her. Or her son. And you said the baking phase only takes a few days. This guy might kill her once she's done cooking this painting!"

Iris studied the townhouse. What if tomorrow was too late? There didn't seem to be any way for them to get inside to save Luna.

Still, she made no move to start the car. She stared at the steam rising from the dryer vent as a thought took shape.

She blew out a breath. It was a crazy idea, really risky. But could it work?

CHAPTER 54

SMOKE ALARMS

As Iris explained her plan to Ash, his eyes grew wide. "But this could get Luna killed!"

"Or it could set her free. We'll call 9-1-1 as soon as the alarms go off." Iris hesitated. She didn't want to be making these life-and-death decisions for a captive stranger. Why wasn't she at home sitting on her sofa with her dog, quietly reading a book? "It's your call, Ash. This is just an idea. We can always wait, and hope that Stroud gets a warrant tomorrow."

"I wish we could see what's happening behind those drapes." Ash's head sank to his chest as he thought. Several moments crept by. Finally, he pulled himself up in his seat. "Screw it. We need to get Luna out of there tonight. Will you do this, or should I?"

"I'll do it." Iris turned to the back seat and grabbed a grubby black towel that she used to keep Sheba's muddy paw prints and slobber off the upholstery.

Ash cracked open his window. They waited while a woman walked briskly by the car, her heels clicking against the brick sidewalk. She rounded the corner onto Mount Vernon Street and disappeared down the hill. No one else was visible around the small square on this freezing Saturday night.

Iris glanced up at the quarter moon, partially hidden behind a cloud, and shivered. Was this going to work? She opened and shut the car door gently, carrying the towel under her arm. Standing on the sidewalk, the security camera on the townhouse wall was in her peripheral vision. She hugged the side of the front staircase, hopefully too close for the camera's rotation to follow. When she reached the dryer vent, which smelled of warm varnish, she reached up and stuffed the towel inside, making sure no fumes could escape around the edges. Then she turned and walked back to the car.

"How long will it take?" Ash asked nervously, his voice low.

"Depends on the last time they had their vents cleaned. Are you ready to make the call?"

"Yeah." Ash's mouth was set in a grim line. "You ready to phone Stroud?"

"Roger that." Iris wondered how close the nearest fire station was. She checked on her phone's browser. Around the corner on Cambridge Street, pretty close. "Let's wait five more minutes before we call." She noted the time. Her plan relied on the occupants of the basement not noticing the smoke entering the room right away and moving to another room to escape it, giving them time to hide Luna.

Ash raised his binoculars to the window.

"Can you see anything with the drapes closed?"

"No."

They suddenly heard smoke alarms blaring from inside the building. "Now!" Ash shouted as he punched in 9-1-1.

Iris ran out of the car and snaked along the staircase to unblock the duct and retrieve the towel. It was probably just smoke, not fire, that set off the alarms, but it had accomplished what she wanted. Now she needed to hide the evidence of her intervention.

Back in the car, she scrolled through her calls and speed-dialed Detective Stroud. "It's Iris. Ash and I are still here at the town-house, and the smoke alarms just went off in the basement. The pizza oven must have overheated or something. We dialed 9-1-1 for the Fire Department, but can you send some officers over or call Boston PD? The firefighters will bring out anyone inside, which hopefully, includes Luna. This may be our chance to get her to safety."

Ash had jumped out of the car and was smashing at the base-ment window between the iron grates with the handle of an umbrella he'd taken from the back seat. He was yelling, "Luna!"

Within several minutes, three fire trucks, four squad cars and two ambulances had parked askew in front of the property. Ash shouted, "The fire's in the basement. My girlfriend's trapped in there!"

The firefighters, seeing grates blocking the basement windows and door, lugged a battering ram from the fire engine up the stairs to the front door. They first tried pounding on it and ringing the doorbell.

Curious residents from adjacent homes came out to watch from their stoops, probably assessing the risk that a developing fire could leap over to their own townhouses. Iris and Ash stood on the sidewalk watching.

An official-looking man in plain clothes pulled Ash aside. "You know how many people are inside?" he shouted.

"My girlfriend—she's in the basement. And two men who were keeping her captive. Don't know about the rest."

"Two men and a woman in the basement!" The man yelled up to the firefighters.

Just as the crew were preparing to ram the front door, it opened. Malik stood there and said calmly, "My housekeeper had a mishap in the basement and set off the alarms. It's under control now. I'm sorry you had to come out for a false alarm."

The basement drapes were now pushed aside, and Iris could see the bald guy opening the two windows to let out streams of smoke. She couldn't see Luna. The alarms were still blaring.

The fire crew chief shouted, "Are you the homeowner?"

"Yes, I am Malik Saban."

The chief said, "We need to go inside to make sure there are no embers still burning in the appliance or anyone with signs of respiratory distress."

Malik stepped aside and directed four firefighters to the stairs leading to the basement.

The chief asked, "Can you please assemble everyone in the house outside on the sidewalk so the EMTs can examine them for smoke inhalation?"

Iris and Ash exchanged looks. Had her plan actually worked?

She peeked in the basement window and could see the bald guy up on a ladder, pressing something on the smoke alarm on the ceiling to try to silence it. A firefighter headed over to the corner with the pizza oven, holding a large flashlight. Others searched the rest of the room for any signs of fire. The alarms suddenly went silent.

A gray-haired woman in a pink tracksuit stumbled out the front door and stepped gingerly down the stairs, holding on to the handrail. Malik followed her, with his hand on her back. An EMT rushed over. "Ma'am, are you alright? Did you breathe in any smoke?"

The woman looked frightened and shook her head. "No English."

"Dilara is my cook," Malik said. "She speaks only Turkish. Her room is at the back of the basement. She wasn't near the smoke."

"We still need to check her out. You too." A medical tech seated

Dilara on the tailgate of the ambulance. He poured her a cup of water and slipped a pulse oximeter on her finger. Another EMT did the same with Malik at the ambulance nearby.

Finally, the bald guy emerged. He walked over to Malik and whispered something in his ear.

Now that Iris could see the second man clearly, she recognized him and nudged Ash. "That's the guy who followed me yesterday!"

"You didn't tell me you were followed. Wait. On Wednesday, Reilly said some guy was spying on us. It might be the same one."

"We'd better be sure they find Luna tonight and arrest these two. Where is she?"

The fire chief called out to the bald guy: "How many more inside?"

"That's everyone."

Both men stared directly at Iris and Ash. One corner of Malik's mouth curved up.

CHAPTER 55
THE TURKISH COOK

Iris glanced over her shoulder to see Detective Stroud talking with a Boston Police detective just as she heard Ash cry out.

"No!" he shouted at the fire chief up on the stoop. "My girlfriend's in there. I just saw her. They're hiding her."

The bald man looked at Ash with narrowed eyes.

"Stroud's here," Iris said to Ash under her breath. "He'll straighten this out."

"Thank God," he muttered, turning to search for the Medford detective.

The Turkish woman in the back of an ambulance was wringing her hands in agitation, darting nervous looks at the neighboring vehicle with Malik inside, an oxygen mask over his lower face. Iris walked over and sat next to Dilara, blocking the cook's view of her boss. Iris took the phone out of her pocket and called up a translation app. She plugged in the words, "Hello, did you see a girl inside?"

Iris had no idea how to pronounce the Turkish, so she showed

Dilara the question on her phone. Merhaba. İçeride bir kız gördün mü?

Dilara grabbed Iris' arm and nodded vigorously. "Evet! Evet!" she said in a hushed voice.

That meant yes, Iris learned. She quickly typed another question about whether Dilara knew where the girl was hidden.

Again, Dilara grabbed the phone to type in her answer in Turkish. She held it up for Iris to see the English translation: I think in the closet in the basement workshop. Iris smiled at her and found the Turkish for: Thank you. You are very brave before rushing over to Detective Stroud and Ash. Before she could speak, Ash blurted out, "Malik's refusing permission for the police to search the house without a warrant."

Iris held up her hand in a stop gesture and murmured, "The cook just told me this." She backtracked to Dilara's last message and showed them the screen. "Since this hiding place is in the basement where the smoke originated from, wouldn't the firefighters need to search that entire floor thoroughly to make sure no smoke or sparks traveled through the wiring or the ductwork?"

"Good point," Stroud said. "Let me speak to the fire chief."

Ash looked over at Dilara and gave her a look of gratitude.

"Don't look at her!" Iris said sharply. "We don't want Malik to know she told us anything. It's dangerous for her."

Ash rubbed the back of his neck. "That was sick, using a translation app. Do you think Luna's alright? Would they have hurt her before shoving her in some closet?"

"They didn't have much time. They probably tied her up and pushed her in, planning to drag her out after the fire guys left." *Unless she'd already inhaled too much smoke and my dangerous plan killed her.* Iris wished the firefighters would hurry and get Luna out of there and into the care of the EMTs.

"God, I hope she's okay," Ash said, his eyes glued to the front door where the Boston detective and Stroud stood together, conferring.

Malik pulled off his oxygen mask and climbed out of the ambulance. He looked up at the detectives and asked, "Can I return to my house now? It appears that all danger is over."

The Boston detective called down to him. "It shouldn't be much longer, sir. The fire crew just needs to check out the ductwork and wiring, make sure nothing was damaged."

The bald guy approached Malik and whispered again in his ear.

Meanwhile, Iris pulled up on her phone the floor plan of the basement she had copied from the building department's files. She studied a large space in the rear next to the tiny suite labeled as a maid's room. Was this where Malik's workshop was now? What was that small room off of it?

Three firefighters and their chief emerged from the entry. The fire chief shook his head at the Boston detective. Iris watched his lips as he formed the words, "No closet off the workshop."

CHAPTER 56
A SECRET ROOM

L una awoke to a slight smell of smoke in a small, dimly lit room. Her pulse raced when she realized she was tied to a chair, her hands behind her back. Her ankles were also taped together. She could barely breathe through the rag tied around her mouth, and her lungs were burning. By pushing the rag several times with her tongue, she was able to lower it on one side. Finally! A little air. She took some ragged breaths.

How long had she been here? Luna remembered getting her dinner that evening and making eye contact with the woman who delivered it. She thought she detected a look of sympathy from her. Luna had specified that the oven be preheated to 248 degrees, and Goran soon brought her down to the basement laundry room. Malik was there too. He carried in both paintings—the original and her copy, ready to be varnished and baked. If both men intended to watch over her for the entire three-hour session, she'd have little chance of escaping.

Malik had reacted to something he'd seen out the window, and Luna followed his glance to see a silhouette of a man on the sidewalk. For one crazy second, she thought it was Ash coming to rescue her. Like that would ever happen. Malik immediately pulled the curtains closed and glared at Goran for his oversight.

But the minute she opened the oven door, smoke billowed out and quickly filled the room. That was the last thing she remembered. No wait, there was a piercing sound–smoke alarms. Did that attract anyone's attention outside? Maybe there were firefighters inside the townhouse now who could help her.

"I'm in here!" she tried to scream. "Can anybody hear me? Help!" Her throat felt scratchy, and her voice was hopelessly muffled.

She needed to get herself out of these restraints. She looked down at her ankles. The blue wrapping looked like painter's paper tape. If there hadn't been so many layers, it would have been easy to rip off. Goran or Malik probably used the same tape around her wrists. Stretching her hands apart, she felt the tape give a little. She twisted their position so the fingers on her right hand could scrape the tape on her left wrist. After a moment, she got her nail under a layer of tape and ripped it across, creating an end she could pull on. She was able to stretch out the restraints even wider and unwrap a layer. Within a few minutes of maneuvering, she'd gotten her hands free. She yanked off the rag partially covering her mouth. It took only a few more moments to free her ankles.

Luna had to get out of here to find Paul. Was he okay? What had Malik done to him? No thinking about that now. She needed to focus on escaping from this room. She stood up shakily to examine her surroundings. The door in front of her was flush with the wall. She tried the knob, but it was locked from the outside. She banged on it. "I'm in here!" she shouted. No sound came through. She flipped on a light switch to help her see better. But when she turned around to study the rest of the room, she froze.

Spotlights illuminated three paintings and an empty easel. She moved closer. The first one looked like a freaking J.M.W. Turner! No other painter captured that hazy, atmospheric light on turbulent waves the way Turner did. She picked up the canvas and held it closer to the light, examining its texture and varnish. This was an original Turner, she'd bet on it. And it was worth a fortune. Malik wouldn't have kept a copy, no matter how good.

Papa, I wish you could see this.

She replaced the Turner carefully on its easel and moved on to the pastel pointillist one. A Seurat, another masterpiece, although not her taste. Too pretty. Luna recognized the third painting immediately of a woman in a bonnet. She'd always believed that Mary Cassatt was underrated. But she had no time to linger over these treasures.

Now she noticed that the Sargent and her copy had been propped up against the wall by the door. Malik must have been pretty damned panicked to have stashed her in with his private collection. So, someone must have responded to the loud smoke alarms. Were they still inside the townhouse?

Luna picked up the chair and pounded it against the door.

CHAPTER 57

ASH, IT'S YOU?

Three men encircled Iris by the front door to study her phone. She had enlarged the floor plan of the basement workshop space and its adjacent room. Ash watched them anxiously from the bottom of the stairs, where Stroud had told him to wait.

"We didn't see any door into that space. There are bookcases all along that wall," the fire chief said.

"The door could be hidden. The type where you press a certain button, or pull down the right book, and it pops open," Iris said.

Stroud, the Boston detective, and the Fire Chief all scowled down at Malik, who was facing away from them talking on his phone, probably to his lawyer.

"What is this guy with the secret rooms—some kind of spy?" The Fire Chief asked.

"We need to figure that out," Stroud said. "And now, with a statement from the cook that she saw a woman being hidden in a closet off the workshop, we have probable cause to enter and

233

search. This floor plan confirms that the room exists. I suggest we pull the shelving away from the wall and look for a way in."

"Do you want me to come along to give architectural input?" Iris asked.

"No, you don't have permission to enter the house. The police do only because we got this tip." The three men and Iris avoided glancing over at Dilara. Stroud had stationed a uniformed police officer near her in case Malik caught on that she had made herself understood in English.

Two firefighters rushed up the front steps carrying flathead axes. The chief said, "We'll get through that wall one way or the other."

WHILE THEY WAITED, EYES RIVETED ON THE FRONT DOOR, IRIS ASKED Ash, "Where is Luna's son? That guy who looks like a thug said there's no one else in the house. Do you think they took Paul away somewhere?"

Ash winced. "That would be torture to take a kid from his mother. I guess when they find Luna, the police will have cause to search the whole place. Paul could be on an upper floor."

Iris glanced over at Malik. Who was this monster? He looked so urbane and civilized in an elegant suit and expensive haircut, talking on his phone. How did he justify kidnapping a woman and child? Iris could never understand what criminals believed about themselves. She hoped to God that Luna and Paul were alive and would be able to recover from this trauma.

A text chirped on Iris' phone. She tipped her head to the side in surprise at the sender. Luc had taken the time on his busiest night at the restaurant to ask,

< Did you find Luna? >

Iris answered,

< We saw her inside through window, but the bad guy hid her. Police are searching now. >

He wrote back,

< Good. Keep your head down. Ash too! >

Iris heard one firefighter say to another, "You should have seen all the lint in that dryer vent. No wonder it smoked when they hooked up an oven to it. Coulda started a fire any minute. And why is there an oven in the laundry room, anyway?" They both shook their heads.

Ash ran up the stairs as the fire chief emerged from the entry carrying Luna in his arms. Her eyes were closed.

"Luna!" Ash called out, rushing to her side.

Her eyes opened, and she murmured, "Ash? Is it really you?" She held out a hand to touch him. Her voice was raspy, and Ash leaned closer as he followed them down the stairs. "Please find Paul. Find my son."

The fire commander took Luna to the EMTs, and they strapped an oxygen mask over her mouth. Ash hovered nearby until the EMTs shooed him away and closed the back door of the ambulance.

"Where are you taking her?" Ash cried out. A police officer said, "They'll head to the Mass General emergency room. Closest hospital, five minutes away."

Stroud stomped out of the townhouse, lips curled in anger and headed straight for Malik. He grabbed Malik's hands roughly and zip-tied them behind his back. "I'm arresting you for the kidnapping of Luna Esposito and her son, Paul. More charges may be brought later." He recited the Miranda warning. Alongside him, the Boston detective repeated the procedure with the bald guy.

Both men were ushered into the back seat of separate police cruisers, and the doors slammed closed behind them.

Iris asked Stroud, "What about the boy? Was he in the townhouse?"

"Several officers are still searching the house, but Ms. Esposito thinks they took him off-site. We're checking real estate records to see if Mr. Saban owns any other properties." Stroud's eyebrows arched up. "You wouldn't happen to know anything about how that fire started, would you?"

Iris gave him her most innocent look. "According to the firefighters, it was lint buildup in the dryer vent. It's a terrible hazard."

After texting Luc that they had found Luna, Iris turned to Ash, who was staring vacantly at the ambulance's path. "Come on. I'll drive you to Mass General."

CHAPTER 58

GABRIELA PETRUCCI

Iris waited at the hospital with Ash until, an hour later, Luna was wheeled out of the emergency room on a gurney. She appeared to be sedated. Ash pretended to be Luna's fiancé so the ER doctor would agree to talk with them.

"We'll need to monitor Ms. Esposito's vital signs overnight to make sure she doesn't have carbon monoxide poisoning. Her throat is raw but not swollen, so we won't need to intubate, but the tissue damage from the gag could lead to infection. Come back tomorrow morning. She should be able to talk to you then."

In the car, driving back to the loft, Ash asked. "Do you think we did the right thing—creating all that smoke? Luna looks in bad shape."

Iris' hands tightened on the steering wheel. "If we hadn't done that, Luna would still be Malik's prisoner."

"Right, you're right. Sorry. It was a good plan and thank God she's safe now. I just hope Paul's okay. Luna wants me to find him. How am I supposed to do that?"

Iris turned the car onto the MIT bridge, crossing the Charles

River back to Cambridge. "Stroud said they were looking to see if Malik owned any other properties. We can call the detective when we get back to the loft to see if he's found anything. Why don't you stay in our guest room tonight since you'll want to head back over to the hospital first thing in the morning."

"Thanks. I'll take you up on that. I'm beat."

Iris pulled into the parking lot behind her building, taking the slot next to Ash's car. Music and voices spilled from the busy first-floor restaurant. The Saturday night dinner service was in full swing.

They climbed the stairs to the second-floor loft. She flipped on the lights, and they headed to the living room to relax.

Iris gave Sheba her undivided attention before sitting on the sofa. Her phone pinged with a text. Kelly wrote,

< My agency discovered information about Luna Esposito. Have you found her? Call me when you get a chance. >

Iris wondered what Kelly was doing working on a Saturday night. She hoped her friend had a social life. It would be around five PM West Coast time, so maybe she still had plans for the evening.

"Hey," Iris said to Ash. "This text is from my friend at Interpol, the one who suggested Luna's father might have been the forger connected to the Petrucci crime family." Iris angled her screen to show him Kelly's message. "Do you want to know what she's learned, or would you rather hear it from Luna? It may be tough information."

Ash, slumped in an armchair, massaged his shoulder. "Might as well find out who I've fallen for."

Kelly picked up right away.

"We found Luna," Iris told her. "She was in that Beacon Hill townhouse I told you about. I'm here with Luc's son, Ash. He's, uh,

238

involved with her and wants to know what you've found out. I'll put this on speakerphone, okay?"

"I guess so. Hi Ash—" Kelly paused. "I'm not sure what Luna told you, but her name is really Gabriela Petrucci."

Ash's expression was stricken. "You mean Luna is part of a mafia family and has two aliases? She's some kind of criminal?"

"We don't think so," Kelly said. "Her uncle Marco is head of the Providence, Rhode Island crime family, but there's no evidence that Luna has ever done anything unlawful."

Ash's shoulders relaxed visibly. "Then why does she keep changing her name?"

"We think she was trying to get away from her Petrucci uncle. He's a dangerous guy—into drugs, trafficking, gambling, extortion, you name it. About twenty years ago, the family added art theft and forgery to their activities. Gabriela's father, Dante, Marco's younger brother, was a gifted portrait painter who became their master forger."

"But she always talked about her father with such admiration," Ash said.

"Our informants implied Dante didn't go along with the family's art business willingly. Marco might have made him one of those deals he couldn't refuse. Still, Dante's forgeries were such accurate replicas that we could never prove they were fakes. Two identical paintings by an Old Master would turn up at auctions in different countries, and no one could tell which one was real."

"We heard Dante died two years ago, and that's when Luna, or Gabriela, moved to Boston," Iris said. "Is it possible that her uncle was pressuring her to take over his position as the family forger? That might be why she was trying to hide her identity and start a new life."

"We won't really know any of those details until we can talk with her," Kelly said. "I've been in touch with our counterparts at the FBI's Organized Crime Unit, and they want to interview her as well. Her father was shot, and his remains were found buried on a construction site in Cranston, R.I. last year. The Petrucci family knew that Gabriela had disappeared and were looking for her. Along with Dante were the remains of a young man identified as Joey Ciampa. They had both been shot at close range. Word was that Ciampa had been dating Dante's daughter."

"That must have been when Luna ran north and changed her name." Ash's voice was low. "This Joey guy must be Paul's father."

There were some moments of silence before Kelly said, "At any rate, my colleague at Interpol and the FBI team want to talk with Gabriela now that she's safe. Not only does she have information about the Petrucci family, but now there's this second forgery ring that she got dragged into. We need to find the artwork that Malik Saban stole while returning forged replicas to the owners or museums. My agency's been looking for this guy for several years."

"But won't this be dangerous for her? Especially if she testifies against the mafia. They could come after her."

"The FBI says it has a plan to protect her."

CHAPTER 59

ASH-SUNDAY

The next morning, when Ash arrived at the door of Luna's hospital room, a police officer was guarding it. "Name and ID please?" the officer asked.

Ash produced both and was relieved to learn he was on the list of approved visitors.

Luna was propped up in bed, staring at her phone. Machines nearby monitored her heart rate, beeping at a steady pace. She was hooked up to an IV but looked noticeably better than she had the night before.

Ash entered shyly, holding out the tulips he'd bought in the first-floor gift shop. "Hey, there."

She tucked the phone beside her in the sheets and stared straight at the flowers, avoiding his eyes. "How did you ever find me?" Her voice was still hoarse.

He set the vase on a table and sat in the chair next to her bed. "I asked someone who's good at tracking people down. We didn't give up 'til we found you." He leaned forward. "Has there been any word about your boy? I got a Medford detective involved in the search, and he's looking for other properties Malik Saban might own, some place where he might be hiding Paul."

"Detective Stroud was here earlier this morning. He brought me my phone and told me Malik owns a house out on Nantucket. Stroud spoke to the police chief out there, who's sending officers to search the property. I'm waiting to hear back from him."

She picked up her phone to check again for messages, then placed it down next to the flowers. She finally looked at Ash. "I have to believe Paul's still alive. Malik was using my son to force me to keep painting for him."

Ash shook his head. "Bastard."

Luna motioned for Ash to sit on the side of the bed. "Look, there's so much I didn't tell you. I'm sorry. I didn't want to put you in danger. My family..." She pulled the sheets up to her neck as if she were cold.

"The Petruccis, right?" Ash responded. "I know about them."

"Yeah, but it's not what you think. Okay, my mother died in childbirth, and my father raised me. He wanted nothing to do with his brother and the rest of the family business. He had tons of talent, but he couldn't make a living painting portraits and seascapes. Uncle Marco recognized his skill and talked him into producing forgeries for him. That allowed Papa to buy a little house and to support the two of us. He also wanted to put money aside for my future, so I could go to college or art school. Papa warned me to stay away from Uncle Marco's world."

Luna raised her hand and stopped talking to check her phone again. "Nothing yet from Nantucket." She put it down on the bed and continued. "I never had many friends. Kids heard my last name and were scared off, so I spent a lot of time at home watching my father paint. He gave me lessons and was proud of my ability. But when I was a teenager, things changed. I had other interests and wanted to hang out with my friends, so I didn't notice Papa's condition right away. He was starting to shake, the Parkinson's taking hold, but I thought he was just getting old."

He could see her jaw working to contain her emotions.

"That was when he told me about the money he'd saved in a safe behind our kitchen cabinets and told me to remember the combination. He made me promise never to use my artistic ability to paint forgeries."

Ash laced his fingers through hers. "You didn't have a choice."

Luna gave a minute shrug. "I should have been a better daughter and listened to him. Papa hated my boyfriend, Joey, so we met behind his back. Big surprise, I ended up getting pregnant."

Ash thought about his mother being in the same boat in high school.

"On an afternoon when Papa told me he would be at the doctor's, Joey and I were up in my room trying to work out some way to be teenage parents. We heard the front door open and voices below—my father and Uncle Marco. They were arguing in the living room. My uncle said if my father couldn't continue producing new forgeries, if his hands shook too much, I would have to do it. My father shouted back that he would never allow me to be dragged into the family business."

Ash gave her hand a small squeeze.

"Joey and I watched from the top landing. We saw Marco pull out a gun. Joey roared and flew down the stairs to try to save my father, but Marco shot them both." The last words came out as sobs.

A few moments later, Luna collected herself and continued. "I crawled out my bedroom window as fast as I could and hid in the woods nearby. Two of my uncle's 'soldiers' drove up and took away the bodies of my father and boyfriend. I knew they would come looking for me next."

"Did you think about telling all this to the police?"

"No. This was Rhode Island. Any number of the cops were on my uncle's payroll."

"So, you took the money from the safe, bought a new identity, and headed up to Boston."

"Yeah. And five months later, I had baby Paul to take care of."

CHAPTER 60
HOSTAGE SITUATION

Iris reached for her second double espresso shot just as Luc thundered up the stairs.

"Didn't you say this morning that the bad guy Malik has a house in Nantucket and the Medford cop thought Luna's son was being held there?"

"Yeah. Why? What's going on?"

"Turn on the TV. The local news. I heard it on the radio driving back from the farmer's market: some woman in Nantucket is holding a kid hostage. The cops have surrounded the house, but she won't let the boy go unless they get her a helicopter or some crazy demand like that."

"Oh, my God!" Iris ran into the living room, closely followed by Luc and Sheba. She grabbed the remote control and punched buttons.

The flat TV screen came alive with breaking news, and the chyron screamed across the bottom: *Hostage Situation in Nantucket.* Local police officers in body armor, as well as State Police in labeled windbreakers, were talking into handheld radios. They had surrounded a weathered shingle-style house, which stood isolated in a large yard of native grass.

The TV camera panned way out. A newscaster in a bulky parka and a watch cap shivered in front of the police barrier outlined by crime scene tape. A brisk wind blew her long blond hair sideways. "We've learned that this house in the Polpis area of Nantucket belongs to Malik Saban, a Boston art appraiser. Inside, a young boy is being held hostage. Mr. Saban was arrested last night for kidnapping the boy's mother, who is now free and recovering in a Boston hospital." The newscaster flashed a sad, concerned look. "The abductor is an employee of Mr. Saban. We've learned that her first name is Helen. She is holding a three-year-old boy hostage at gunpoint and demanding a helicopter to take her to an undisclosed location. She will release the boy only when the aircraft arrives."

"Shouldn't the FBI and a SWAT team be there?" Iris asked. "The Nantucket police are probably more used to breaking up rowdy parties or chasing off kids messing around in the dunes."

"No time," Luc pulled his chair closer to the screen. "To get them organized and out there on helicopters would take several hours. The Staties have a small barracks on the island, so the local cops must have pulled them in."

Iris couldn't help smiling as Luc morphed from chef to son of a Cambridge cop. She wished she had met his father, Scott Cormier.

"I hope Luna isn't watching this!" Iris grabbed her phone and texted Ash.

< Are you still with Luna? Don't let her turn on the TV! >
Ash texted back,
< Why not? Have they found Paul? He's not... >
Iris considered what to say.
< No! He's alive but on Nantucket. The police are trying to get him away from the woman who's got him. I'll let you know as soon as he's safe. >

< Luna's waiting for a call from Stroud. Not sure what he'll say. I should tell her Paul's okay. >

< OK—use your judgement. >

Iris hit send and turned her attention back to the windblown reporter on the screen.

"We don't know the identity of the mother—"

Good luck with that, Iris thought, considering Luna's various assumed identities.

"... or why Malik Saban was holding her against her will. Our focus now is on the young child who is being held in the house behind me. You can see the negotiator from the Mass State Police's Special Tactical Operations Team, known as STOP, trying to de-escalate the stand-off."

The camera zoomed in on the back of a man with MSP embla-zoned on his windbreaker, standing by a police van, hunched over a phone.

"If there's only one woman holding Paul, why can't the police just shoot her through a window?" Iris asked.

"The STOP team probably has a sharpshooter, but he might not be able to see her if the curtains are closed. Or he can't get a clear shot if she's holding Paul close to her."

"This is nerve-wracking. I really hope Luna isn't watching this. I'm having a heart attack, and I've never even met the poor kid."

"Stroud may need to ask Luna if she knows anything about this Helen person that can help the negotiators," Luc said. "But that would require telling her that Paul's a hostage."

"Look!" Iris pointed at the screen. "That officer on the left. He's edging over to the window and crouching. He's lifting his rifle!"

"Shooting's a last resort if there's a hostage. Especially a kid."

The sound of shattering glass and the blast of a rifle report reverberated from the TV.

Iris sucked in a breath.

All the law enforcement officers on the screen started talking at once or listening to their handheld devices. Then the officer who had fired the shot used his rifle butt to clear the lower window sash of glass and reached in to turn the lock. He raised the sash and scrambled inside.

A few moments later, he appeared at the front door carrying a terrified little boy in his arms. Paul blinked at the bright camera lights and let out a wail.

Iris texted Ash.

< Paul is safe! >

CHAPTER 61

ASH-SUNDAY

Ash was sitting on the side of Luna's hospital bed when her phone rang with a call from Detective Stroud. She put it on speaker so Ash could hear.

"Paul is safe!" Stroud said. "A Nantucket police sergeant is bringing your son to Mass General now by helicopter. Paul appears to be in good shape. They'll bring him to your room after doing some preliminary tests. He should be there in a little over an hour."

"Oh, thank God! Thank you, detective." Luna whispered before ending the call. She was trembling.

Ash held her close as sobs racked her slender body. When Luna pulled away, her eyes were puffy and her skin blotchy. "He's alive. That's all that matters. I'll never forget that you helped us escape, Ash. I'm so grateful." She gave him a gentle hug.

"It's going to be alright now," Ash said. "You're both safe. Why don't you come back to the studio with Paul? You can paint your own work again and won't have to worry about anyone coming after you."

Luna's expression grew serious. "We'll never be safe with my uncle still looking for me. I saw him shoot Papa and Joey. That hasn't changed."

They both jumped at the sharp knock on the door. A tall man in a grey suit stood in the doorframe. He identified himself as an FBI agent. An agent with a black pixie haircut followed him in and offered her own ID for Luna to inspect.

"Ms. Petrucci, we'd like to speak with you privately."

Luna startled at hearing that long-discarded name but nodded. Ash rose and left the room.

THE TEA STOPPED DRIPPING OUT OF THE VENDING MACHINE NOZZLE. Ash picked up the Styrofoam cup and sniffed the liquid. It smelled suspiciously like the coffee dispensed from the same machine. He probably wouldn't drink it anyway. He just wanted to stretch his legs while he waited for the FBI agents to leave and avoid making awkward small talk with the police officer guarding Luna's room.

After forty minutes, her door finally opened, and the agents walked out, avoiding Ash's eyes as they passed.

He poked his head into the room. "Okay if I come in, or do you need to rest?"

Luna gestured him in. She looked drawn and nervous.

Ash sat down again on the side of the bed and laced his fingers through hers. "Did the Feebees want to talk to you about your uncle?"

"Uh-huh. They're from the organized crime unit," Luna said. "I agreed to testify that I saw Marco kill my father and Joey. I need to go on the record and get Uncle Marco off my back for good."

"But even if he's sent to prison, can't your uncle send people after you? It's dangerous."

Luna slipped her hand out of his. "What's my choice, Ash? I can't keep hiding. That life isn't good for Paul or for me."

Several moments of silence elapsed before she caught his eye. "I'm sorry Ash, but I need to go away. Someplace far away where no one knows me, and we can feel safe."

CHAPTER 62

TWICE LOST

The day after Luna vanished into the fog of the Witness Protection Program, Iris invited Ash over for dinner. She was worried about how he was taking the loss. Luc's restaurant was closed on Mondays, and she'd volunteered to cook for the three of them.

Before Ash arrived, Iris took the fragrant ratatouille out of the oven to rest. "How did he seem when you talked yesterday?"

"Lost, totally lost." Luc said. "I wish I could help him."

Was Luc remembering his own despair when, twenty-two years ago, Ash's mother had abruptly disappeared from Luc's life?

The intercom let out a loud chirp.

"I'll get it." Luc jogged down the stairs. Iris could hear him talking with his son in the entryway. The two of them climbed up a moment later, and Sheba wriggled in excitement to see Ash. He came into the kitchen to give Iris a hug.

As he pulled away, she saw the shattered look in his eyes. He seemed more vulnerable than Iris had ever seen him. She noticed he now wore a Greek coin on a black cord around his neck. *The Athena necklace Kiera said Luna always wore.* A memento.

"You holding up?" Iris asked.

"I don't know." Ash rubbed harshly at his brow as though trying to wake himself from a bad dream. "At least I've gotten rid of Kevin the cat. He meowed like crazy when he saw Luna. Didn't give me a second glance when she carted him off."

Luc rested a hand on Ash's shoulder and handed him a stein of beer. "Let's go sit in the living room."

Iris grabbed her wineglass and joined them. Spotting Monday's *Boston Globe* still lying on the coffee table, she snatched it up and took it back to the recycling bin in the kitchen.

The press had enjoyed a field day with Luna's and Paul's dramatic escapes, leaving out any mention of involvement by Iris or Ash. The bigger story, still on the front page, was about the art appraiser who had kidnapped Luna and her son to coerce her into forging paintings. This was something new. The public had pretty much shrugged off the side story of the discovery that a mob boss had murdered Luna's father and boyfriend several years ago. Isn't that what mob bosses did? Although they rarely did their own dirty work.

Wagging her tail, Sheba hiked herself up onto the sofa next to Ash, and he scratched her behind the ears. "I spoke with Luna before she left. Paul still isn't talking. He'll need therapy to get over the trauma Malik Saban put him through, but Luna can't take the chance of having Paul reveal any of this in their new location." He let out a dry laugh. "Wherever that is. I never even got to meet the kid."

Ash lifted his eyes and met Iris'. His pained look spoke paragraphs. Whole pages.

Iris felt a sudden, deep fury at these men, the damned uncle and then Malik, who had stolen a chunk of Luna's and Paul's life and, by extension, Ash's. She hoped that those two devils would be locked up for the rest of their miserable lives.

Luc asked, "Will she come back to testify in the separate trials when the time comes?"

"They said she could do it remotely." Ash blew out a breath. "It's easy for the Feds to say they can hide Luna, and she can start a new life. But her style of painting is distinctive. I don't care what kind of cage they put her uncle in. Unless she gives up painting, or totally changes her style, the Petrucci goons will track her down through her art. They'll want revenge for her testimony against Marco."

Iris' heart sank. Bad enough that Luna and Paul had to uproot themselves once more. But not to be able to use your creative talent? She couldn't imagine that.

None of them had much of an appetite for dinner.

Ash ate half of his ratatouille and didn't touch his salad. After Iris and Luc finished their main course, Ash placed his napkin on the table. "I'm sorry, Iris. I'm not doing your cooking justice. Is it okay if I pass on dessert? I don't have much appetite, and I need to go home and lie down. It's been a hell of a last few days."

He carried his plate to the kitchen, and Luc walked him downstairs and out to his car.

Back inside, Luc walked up behind Iris, who was scrubbing a pan at the sink. "Let me do that."

"I should never have gotten involved." Iris handed him the scrub brush. "Ash wouldn't have had to go through losing Luna twice."

"But then she and her son would still be prisoners, or maybe dead. This way, they have a second chance for a decent life."

Iris looked at Luc, her brows raised. "You're saying you *approve* of my getting involved in these kinds of things, these crimes?"

Luc lay the pan back down in the sink. "You brought two real villains to justice when law enforcement couldn't. And I appreciate your helping Ash find Luna. It wasn't the resolution he wanted, but the Petruccis had been hunting for Luna before Ash even met her. You couldn't have changed that outcome." Luc rested his hands on Iris' hips. "Plus, you managed to accomplish all that without putting yourself or Ash in any danger, for once."

Iris rested her forehead on his broad chest. She guessed this wasn't the time to mention that Malik Saban's henchman, the bald guy who'd just been arrested, had been stalking her and Ash. Or that if Dilara the cook hadn't given the police critical information when she did, Malik and Goran might still be on the loose and coming after Ash and her. And Luna might be dead.

EPILOGUE
ASH-THREE MONTHS LATER

Ash took two steps back to better view the large canvas on the Bibi Rosenthal Gallery's otherwise stark white wall in Boston's South End. The ghostly pentimento of Vermeer's *Girl with a Pearl Earring* was barely visible under the dozen overlapping layers of dark wash Ash had applied. Did it resemble the rest of Luna's series? Had he managed to forge the forger's style?

"It's half an inch too low on the right." Ash called to Derek, the snotty gallery assistant. "A little higher. Yes, that's it."

Derek set a level on top of the picture frame, just to make the point of second-guessing Ash's eyeballed assessment.

On that Saturday evening three months ago, when Ash had last seen Luna, she'd begged him to finish this painting. "You know my technique for building up veils. We've talked about it enough, no?" She had to leave all her artwork behind when she vanished into her new life, but she couldn't stand the idea of leaving her *Prisoner* series incomplete.

"Do whatever you want with them," she'd said, sweeping her hand around her almost-empty studio.

Ash had convinced his own gallery owner to give Luna a show in absentia. He would make sure that the FBI confidentially passed along the commissions from any sales to her.

Do you approve of how I hung your first show, babe? I wish you were here to see it.

Ash ran his fingers up and down the black cord with its gold medallion that he hadn't taken off since Luna hung it around his neck.

DEREK MOVED ON TO THE LOCATION ASH HAD DESIGNATED FOR THE next painting and made a light pencil mark for its centerline sixty inches from the floor. He looked at Ash expectantly, his fist on his hip. "This goes here?"

"That looks right."

Ash turned at the echo of clicking heels on the polished concrete floor. Bibi Rosenthal's snowy crash-helmet hairdo didn't budge as she strode across the large open space. Her severe suit of the day was a dove gray Eisenhower jacket with a voluminous skirt.

"Esposito's paintings look even better than the digital versions. I'm hearing a lot of buzz from the postcards we sent out. Quite a few of my major collectors are coming to the opening night party on Saturday. You're sure we can't get more paintings from her?"

"'fraid not."

Bibi took a large envelope out of the pocket of her skirt and handed it to him. "This came to the gallery addressed to you."

Ash noted that the plain white envelope had no postmark or

stamp. His name was printed in block letters. "How was this delivered?"

"Derek thinks it must have been put through the mail slot overnight. He found it inside the front door when he arrived this morning."

Nice of him to mention it to me.

Bibi drifted over to the painting Derek had hung to inspect it up close.

Ash hesitated briefly before tearing open the envelope. Would Malik be sending him a packet of deadly ricin from prison? But what he found inside was a photo of an elaborate painting. The medium was acrylics, bleeding and speckling in a circular explosion of color. Slashes, dots, and arcs. It seemed to contain layers of meaning. He'd never seen this style before and wanted time to study it.

Ash looked inside the envelope for a letter, some explanation. The photo had nothing written on the back. He studied it again. In the lower corner, he saw the artist's scrawled signature: Kevin.

He burst out laughing. Somehow, Luna knew what he was doing for her at the gallery. And she wanted him to know that she'd found a way, as an artist, to reinvent herself one more time.

AN INDEPENDENT
AUTHOR'S REQUEST

I hope you enjoyed Iris' latest adventure, *The Forger's Daughter*. Please help show your support by leaving a review on the site where you purchased this book. Your comments and reviews are very valuable, and I would love to hear your feedback.

Thank you, and I hope you're looking forward to the next installment in the Iris Reid Mystery Series.

For early notification of further Iris Reid Mystery Series books, please sign up on my webpage: www.susancory.com for my newsletter and a free exclusive story.

Thanks again!

Susan Cory

ACKNOWLEDGMENTS

My gratitude and thanks, as always, goes to my amazing editor Dan Tenney. This book is so much better for your input. A big thank you also to my writing group: Amy Reade, Millie Eidson, and Madeleine Dimond for keeping me more or less on the rails. And a shout-out to my wonderful beta readers who provided valuable insights: Janice Schupak, Barbara Melvoin, Judy Pickerill, Leslie Wheeler, and Denise Dilanni.

Barbara Shapiro's excellent book *The Art Forger* described the technique of achieving a crackling effect to age a canvas and Alex Tzavaras' YouTube videos demonstrated how to imitate John Singer Sargent's painting style. Any mistakes are solely mine.

Finally, I'd like to thank you readers who buy my books and allow me to keep writing.

www.ingramcontent.com/pod-product-compliance
Lightning Source LLC
Chambersburg PA
CBHW070854250626
47159CB00003B/1063